CHILD OF THE DARK STAR

Books by Moyra Caldecott

FICTION
Guardians of the Tall Stones:
The Tall Stones
The Temple of the Sun
Shadow on the Stones
The Silver Vortex

Weapons of the Wolfhound
The Eye of Callanish
The Lily and the Bull
The Tower and the Emerald
Etheldreda
Child of the Dark Star
Hatshepsut: Daughter of Amun
Akhenaten: Son of the Sun
Tutankhamun and the Daughter of Ra
The Ghost of Akhenaten
The Winged Man
The Waters of Sul
The Green Lady and the King of Shadows

NON-FICTION/MYTHS AND LEGENDS
Crystal Legends
Three Celtic Tales
Women in Celtic Myth
Myths of the Sacred Tree
Mythical Journeys: Legendary Quests

CHILDREN'S STORIES
Adventures by Leaflight

CHILD OF THE DARK STAR

by

Moyra Caldecott

Published by
Bladud Books

First published in Great Britain in 1984 by Bran's Head Books

This edition published in 2005 by
Bladud Books, an imprint of
Mushroom Publishing, Bath, UK

www.mushroompublishing.com

ISBN 1-899142-23-1

Printed and Bound by
Lightning Source

Contents

*THERE WAS A PLANET ONCE, CALLED EARTH.
ITS PEOPLE, SCATTERED LIKE SEEDS BEFORE
THE WIND, CAME TO REST ON AGARON . . .*

*Had this moment of destruction come, then, from
such a small beginning? Could even an Astrologer
have foretold that a girl gathering crops in a field,
filled with the love of her unborn child, would lead
to the scene now before him . . .*

Or is there ever a beginning?

*Hope, like a small leaf unfurling from a dark and
wrinkled seed, pushed out from his aching heart . . .
If there is never a beginning will there ever be an
end?*

CHAPTER 1

Untimely Birth

The land lay stained and blotched with shadow. Only the high ground still caught the full rays of the setting star, the Red Star, star of guardians and governors, and of hunters.

Firilla knew that she should go back to the farmhouse before the dread Dark Star swallowed all the light and left the fields, the hills and the valleys in icy desolation. But the zorrel crop was good, and her foster-father Bridin needed all the coin he could earn to build the new barn he needed. Firilla was with child, her infant due at the next turning of the heavens, when the dark would have left and the glow of the Blue Star would illumine everything with a soft and beautiful light.

'Just one more row,' she thought, 'and I'll go back.'

The soil was already becoming hard and cold and the tough, prickly little plants more difficult to pluck. Her hands were stained with the juice that flowed from their fluted stems, and the hem of her skirt was dusty and full of marra burrs, the seeds of the pesty little weeds that always sheltered under the red zorrel. But she sang as she worked, happy to think that her child, conceived at the highest point of the White Star's influence and due to be born under the Blue Star, would have a good chance of being a priest-seer of exceptional ability.

She was smiling when a chill shadow touched her.

She looked up startled, the smile fleeing from her eyes. A giant garrar beast was there, hovering immediately above her, its huge wingspread cutting out what was left of the light, the heat of its breath scorching her skin.

She screamed and ran, dropping her load, stumbling over the furrowed field, the zorrel thorns catching at her legs. She tripped, and in steadying herself found a sharp stone which she seized and flung with all her might at the winged beast. It must have struck home, for the creature shrieked. Firilla scrabbled frantically for another sharp stone. The garrar was wounded, and it was angry.

It swooped, and Firilla, with the strength of a mother desperate to protect her young, rammed a stone into the creature's beak as it opened to tear at her. But as she turned, feverishly trying to avoid its claws, the weight of the child within her making her clumsy and slow, the talons closed over her and the garrar lifted to the sky in triumph, Firilla gripped in its claws.

With extraordinary clarity, as though the pain and the terror had sharpened her senses, she saw the landscape slide beneath her: crop-fields in neat triangular segments spreading from the central villages like spokes of vast wheels, and outside the cultivated circles the wild, waiting-to-reclaim-the-land tangled forests of tree-garths, their branches interlaced so tightly to feed off each other that no light reached the ground and only blind creatures hunting by dark could survive. Occasional flashes hurt her eyes as the wheeling flight of the garrar caused her to catch the reflection of the dying star in the smooth mirror of the waterways. But these soon disappeared as the open land disappeared. Beyond the forest, even darker and more sinister, a ridge of jagged mountains rose. For the villagers they had always been a source of legend, a place of thunder, remote and inaccessible – and Firilla saw with horror that her captor was making straight for them.

Strangely, she could hardly feel the pain now, nor see as clearly. It was as though darkness was rapidly spreading from the huge circle of the horizon until her vision constricted to one small brilliant point, and then that, in its turn, was snuffed out.

She did not see the scarlet figure of the hunter as he drew

the gut string back and aimed his shaft, nor did she sense the rush of air as the wood and metal found its mark; only the spin and spiral as the garrar fell, still tenaciously gripping her.

Swiftly the hunter sent another arrow to the garrar's heart, and then, sure that it was dying, climbed down the cliffside from where he had first seen the beast and its burden. Precariously he held to root and outcrop, finding hand and footholds where he could. When he reached them the garrar was dead, its slimy blood soaking the soil. Mercifully the girl had been flung free in the beast's last convulsive twitching and was lying some distance from the body, her fall broken by a mezmer bush, most of its white puff-balls snapped clear and filling the air with a miasma of fine seed-dust.

The young hunter, barely able to control the nausea caused by the smell of the garrar's blood, and afraid that the hallucinogenic effect of the mezmer seeds would get to him and destroy his resolve and sap his strength, dragged the girl hastily clear, ripping her clothes on branches as they went. She was bleeding badly and several bones were clearly broken, but she was alive.

He lifted her over his shoulder and staggered off, determined not to stop until he was out of sight and up-wind of both the carcass and the debilitating seeds. He knew the garrar's mate might well be near and all his skill as bowman and strength as a man might be needed.

At last he found a safe place. It was beside a stream, and he bathed the girl's wounds, marvelling at the miracle of her survival. Her hair was harvest colour, brown and red-gold, her lashes long, her nose and mouth, as he wiped the blood from them, small and fine. Through her torn clothes he could see that her body, though at the moment distended with pregnancy, was young and beautiful.

She opened her eyes, staring with amazement into his. For a moment there was no fear, then memory returned. She started, her face darkened, her grey-green eyes anxiously seeking what she dreaded over his shoulder.

'It's dead,' he told her quietly. The shadow lifted from her face as the darkness lifts from the land at the rise of the White Star.

He squatted down beside her. Was it the effect of the mezmer seeds that made him feel as though, looking deeply into her eyes, he had always been with her? Tentatively he put out a hand and brushed a strand of hair from her cheek. She turned her head as though to hide a twinge of pain. The shadows were returning.

'What can I do?' he asked. He could see that she was trying to lift her head, though the effort was almost too much for her. He put his hand at the back of her neck and gently helped her. She looked down at her body. The leather of his shirt had been slit into strips and both her legs were bound to sticks.

'Broken,' he said as she stared at them.

She looked at her torn clothes, the hump of her unborn child. Pain came in a dark and uncontrollable wave, distorting her features. 'What is it?' he asked sharply.

'My child . . .' she whispered. 'My child must not be born now!'

The pain had passed, but she knew what it meant. Her eyes, filled with horror, looked at him, and he understood. The Dark Star's shadows were closing in on them and any child born now would be born under its baleful influence. 'Can't you . . . can't you . . . hold it back?' he cried, though he knew that she couldn't. He could see her lips, almost blue with cold, moving as though she were praying. He broke into a sweat; he was a bowman-hunter born under the Red Star, trained to bring death, not to attend birth. He crouched beside her helplessly as she doubled up with another contraction.

'What must I do?' he pleaded. 'Tell me . . . tell me . . . what must I do?'

'Build fire,' she murmured as the wave of pain spent itself and withdrew. 'Build it close.'

She was shivering in the rags the garrar claws and mezmer

branches had reduced her to, and he had already used his shirt to bind her legs. He set about gathering wood, relieved to have a task, stumbling on the rocks in his haste and the growing dark, never going far from her, returning every few moments to look anxiously at her. The pains were frequent and severe, but she seemed calmer, knowing that what could not be avoided must be faced. The stubborn instinct of the mother, to bring her child to birth no matter what the circumstances, sustained her.

His hands were shaking as he mixed the fire-powders from the two pouches at his belt, and at last flame leapt in the darkness and took the kindling he had gathered.

Suddenly she screamed, unnerving in the silence, and with a last push brought her child into being. It lay between its mother's legs, in darkness, the flickering glow from the fire making a play of grotesque shadows. He stared fascinated, horrified. A child of the Dark Star!

'Help me,' the woman cried, as he did not move. 'Cut and bind the cord. Keep the child warm.' Obediently he did as he was told, gathering the child up, wiping it clean with rags from its mother's dress, and handing it, squalling, into her arms. She wept as she kissed her son's tiny forehead.

The young man stared at her, shaken, doubt in his eyes as he watched her caress.

'You're not going to keep him! Surely you're not thinking of keeping him?' She did not reply, but when he looked into her eyes he knew his answer. 'But . . .' he whispered, 'but . . .' He shivered as the dark stirred dangerously around him.

She looked up beyond the red sparks of the fire that spiralled above them into the vast realms of sky through which those other stars, the distant points of brightness that gave no light to the world, mysteriously and magnificently took their course. Was there no higher court to which she could appeal, beyond the rigid laws of the Seven Stars of Agaron?

'I will keep him!' she whispered fiercely. 'The Lord of Darkness has no right to him.'

The young man, Glidd, was confused. Seeing Firilla propped against a rock, holding with such love the soft and innocent creature at her breast, he found it hard to believe that the boy was destined to become one of the dreaded out-law caste of those born under the Dark Star.

'The White Star of his conception and the Blue Star that was foretold for his birth will hold him in their influence,' she pleaded as Glidd stood silent, wanting to believe that this were possible. The child's actual birth-time had been an accident and it may be that his destiny had already been fixed under the Birth-Star assigned to him. But only an Astrologer would be able to tell them for sure, and decisions had to be made at once.

Glidd walked away from Firilla and wrestled with his conscience. She had been through a great deal and could not be expected to be thinking clearly. He remembered nights at the lodge when he and his friends had discussed just this kind of situation, not dreaming that one of them would be called upon so soon to make an actual decision.

How much easier it had been to talk! He had seen too much of the ravages of bandits, the cruel wantonness of the marsh-dwellers, to rest easy in his mind if he let the child live to grow up as one of these, and yet . . . and yet . . . As a young boy he had been with his father when he had left his own newborn brother to a slow and painful death in the desert . . . No parent who so exposed a child born under the Dark Star considered themselves to be guilty of their death, nor, if the child survived, would accept responsibility for its life.

Glidd paced back and forth as the woman dropped her cheek to the soft head of her child and dozed off. He knew very well what he should do – and to do it quickly would be merciful.

He drew his dagger and approached the sleeping child, but as he drew back his hand to strike, the baby stirred, its tiny fingers uncurling, its mouth pursing, sucking on a dream of milk. Glidd paused, and on that pause the whole shape of the planet's future hung.

Firilla jerked awake, her eyes blazing with extraordinary strength and anger as she saw the knife. No sound was made, but between them at that moment a force that seemed to belong to neither of them was at work.

Glidd tried to bring his knife down upon the child, but he could not. He knew already that it was too late and was startled to catch in the girl's eyes a look of ferocious triumph totally out of keeping with the impression he had formed of her. But even as he caught it, it was gone, and she broke down and wept.

'I'll prevent him from doing harm. I swear it! Let me keep him!'

'How can you swear that?' he said sadly, putting his knife away.

'I will watch him and guide him every moment of his life. I will not let him go to the marshes, nor to the villages or the towns. We will live here in the mountains. No one will know. No one will be harmed.'

He wanted to believe her, but his heart was heavy with foreboding. He bowed his head. 'It is your child. Your decision.'

She dropped her cheek to her child's soft head with relief. 'My prayers will always be with you,' she murmured.

'And mine with you,' he said gently.

He did not leave her alone with her child in the mountains as she requested, but stayed with them and found food for her. He built her a rough shelter against the weather and the smaller wild creatures of the place. When he had seen her settled on her bed of leaves, a store of berries and his freshly filled water bottle beside her, he left her to return to his lodge, promising that he would return with other comforts she would need, and special herbs for her wounds.

For a long time he kept looking back, hesitating to leave her, and she lifted her head, straining to follow him with her eyes until there was no trace of the torch he carried. Only then did she fall back upon the leaves, trying to blink the tears away, not knowing if she would ever see him again, the soft breathing of the baby in her arms the only thing keeping her from despair.

Firilla had never known the fear of darkness so overwhelmingly before. As a child it had always been held at bay by the circle of firelight, by her family and friends gathered round her, by the walls of her home and the thin fabric of her windows. She had shuddered at tales of what happened under the Dark Star, but always from the safety of her home. Now she was vulnerable to it, utterly exposed, the huge rocks of the mountains surrounding her, pressing towards her with their heavy, silent shadows, their dark presence oozing into every chink of her shelter, every pore of her being.

She held the child so tightly she almost squeezed the life from him. Her tears fell on his head. 'Please let him return,' she whispered, shivering, thinking of Glidd.

At last she slept. She woke and suckled her son, and slept again.

How much time passed she could not tell, but at last she heard Glidd calling, and then saw the light he carried. When he was near enough to hold it over her to see her face he was shocked at the desperation he saw. He knelt beside her. 'It's all right,' he murmured. 'It's all right. I'm back. You're safe.'

Safe? With the Dark Star like a huge incubus in the sky above them, and the Lord of Darkness himself abroad and on the prowl?

CHAPTER 2

The Crown of Garrar Feathers

Glidd built Firilla, and the boy they had named Bardek, a sturdy cabin, half against the mountain rock, and half free standing. At first he spent a great deal of time back at the lodge with his friends, but gradually he spent more and more time with Firilla and Bardek, and she made no protest when at last he drew back the furs he had provided for her and climbed into her bed beside her.

Together they watched the growth of Bardek closely, teaching him all that they thought he should know of their planet. The only lie they deliberately told him was that he was conceived under the Green Star of his mother and born under the Red Star of Glidd.

Seemingly all went well, for the boy was bright and quick of eye and mind. Under Firilla's tutoring he learned about the growth and care of plants. In the Long Dark when they stayed indoors as much as possible he listened fascinated to the stories and myths that had been handed down through the generations, some so ancient that they were from that Other Place, Earth, the sad and distant planet that had ceased to be. Together they taught him writing, and sometimes he wrote stories of his own on the parchment Glidd brought back from the city, or painted strange devices on the vellum they had made themselves from the skins of the animals they hunted for food. Bardek learned to make inks from certain plants and to gather the quills dropped by whains. He grew as agile as a mountain creature and soon knew every rock and cranny in the whole range of the Kariva mountain chain, as happy to follow Glidd in the hunt and to fetch what had fallen to his arrow as to work with his mother in the garden or to sit dreaming over an ancient legend.

Firilla watched him time and again set off with Glidd to learn the art of the bowman, content that she had made the right choice in preserving his life, her love for both of them growing every day.

But one day Bardek set off by himself in search of feathers for a new set of arrows he was fletching, and was away so long Firilla began to fret. She pleaded with Glidd to search for him. 'He can't be lost,' said Glidd, 'he knows these mountains better than a fear-all.'

'The Dark is coming.'

Glidd smiled and kissed the top of her head. 'You and the fear-alls have much in common,' he said tenderly. 'I'll have to make you a hat of their white fur, and you can call them brothers.'

'You may mock, but he often dreams when he should be alert. Garrars may be out. He's never been alone in the dark.'

Glidd sighed and fastened on his arrow belt and his bow. The knife he always wore on the hunt he lashed to his leg.

'You may need light if he is far afield,' Firilla called, and rushed to give him a slow burning berga bough and his double pouch of fire powders.

Firilla watched him go and her heart stirred uneasily. She sensed that something was reaching for them that she did not want to face. These days she rarely climbed the ridge to look to the west where the heavy rain fell and the forests of Tree-garths separated her from her former home. She had accepted that she could never see her family and friends again, and contented herself completely with her love for Bardek and for Glidd. The only horizon she looked to was the eastern one, where the city of Bar-geda lay beyond the plains of Marvara. It was there that Glidd sometimes went for provisions or for entertainment. When he was gone, she and Bardek would watch for the tiny plume of dust in the dry landscape that would indicate his return, Bardek as eager for his presence as she was, asking questions without ceasing about the city and what Glidd could be doing there.

As he strode across the mountainside in the deepening shadow, Glidd called the boy, and his voice flicked from rock to rock and then, dying, rumbled underfoot in the cracks and deep hidden caves of the mountain. A furry white fear-all scuttled from almost under his foot, terrified. Above wheeled the feathered whains, crying out to each other, dreading the coming dark.

Bardek did not usually stay out so long, and for all his mocking Glidd was as concerned as Firilla. 'Bardek!' he called. 'Bardek!' But no voice than his own came back to him.

He had determined to give up the search, convincing himself that Bardek must surely have returned home by now, when he came upon him in a place where the rocks formed a natural amphitheatre. There, standing on top of a rock, his arms lifted as though delivering an oration, stood Bardek. On his head was a crown of tall black feathers.

Glidd felt suddenly chilled. The boy was looking at something Glidd could not see and his face was flushed, almost feverish.

'Bardek.' Glidd brought out the name gruffly, but he had to say it three times before the child looked at him, and then he looked puzzled, as though he did not recognise Glidd. Only gradually did the flush leave his face and pleasure come to his eyes.

'Glidd!' he cried, and jumped off the rock.

'What were you doing?' Glidd demanded, trying not to let the anxiety he felt show in his voice.

'I was making a speech,' Bardek said happily. 'I was pretending to be a priest.'

'Priests do not wear crowns of black feathers,' Glidd said sharply.

'Oh,' said Bardek, reaching up and taking the crown from his head, 'I found these. Aren't they beautiful?' He held them up proudly for Glidd to see. The last light caught the surface of their blackness and a kind of red fire seemed to flash from the surface of them. 'They must be garrar feathers, but I never knew they could flash like that,' he said.

The boy looked so cheerful and innocent Glidd was reassured that he was unaware of the significance of a crown of black feathers. 'The garrar is a beast of ill omen. Throw them away, boy, they will do you no good.' Glidd knew that Firilla would instantly see a dark meaning in this incident, and decided not to tell her of it.

'I want to keep them,' protested Bardek. 'They're beautiful.'

'No,' snapped Glidd.

He had never spoken so harshly to the boy before and Bardek looked at him in some surprise. His eyes clouded. 'I want to keep them,' he repeated.

'They will frighten your mother. Throw them away. A garrar did her great harm once.'

'But they are not attached to the garrar. They are just feathers!'

'Nothing is ever *just* anything,' Glidd said firmly. 'Throw them away.'

'I'll hide them here so that mother never sees them, but I'll not throw them away.'

Glidd hesitated. He could see the stubbornness in Bardek's eyes, and he knew that the boy had a kind of strange strength sometimes, in spite of his youth, that he hesitated to challenge. 'All right,' he said unwillingly, thinking that a compromise was better than a defeat, and planning to return without the boy and destroy the crown. He watched carefully as Bardek found a crevice in which to hide his trophy, and marked its position.

'What speech were you making?' he asked curiously as they made their way back to Firilla.

'I can't remember!' the boy laughed. 'Although it seemed a great speech at the time. I was trying to rouse them to some kind of action . . . but what it was I just can't think!'

'Who are "they"?' Glidd asked, stopping to light the torch.

Carefully he took a pinch of the two fire powders, mixed them together on a rock, and lit the berga bough from the sudden flare-up.

'It's a funny thing,' Bardek said thoughtfully. 'I've never seen any people but you and mother and yet . . . and yet . . .'

'And yet what?' Glidd looked at him closely.

'I do see others . . .'

'Where?'

'They just sort of . . . appear and . . . disappear . . .'

'What do they look like?'

'Oh, just people. Different kinds of people.'

'Are you sure you don't fall asleep and dream?'

'It doesn't feel like dreaming.'

'Dreaming very often doesn't!'

'There is always one . . . more important than the rest . . .' said Bardek thoughtfully.

'Describe that one.' Glidd almost held his breath.

'He . . .' The boy's voice trailed away for a moment and there was a frown on his brow. 'It is really strange. Sometimes I feel he is inside me and at other times . . . outside.'

'Does he wear a crown of black feathers?' The anxiety was unmistakable in the man's voice.

Bardek suddenly laughed. 'I just found those old feathers lying about and tied them with a piece of my sandal thong. Why do you make such a fuss about them?'

Glidd bit his lip. He could not tell Bardek of his true Birth-Star and of the dark god who governed those born under it.

As soon as the light began to return Glidd hurried back to the rock amphitheatre. But there was no sign of Bardek's feathers. Glidd stood on the spot where Bardek had made his speech, and looked out towards the plains of Marvara which stretched, in varying shades of blue, to the small blur on the horizon that was the distant city of Bar-geda. Two great columns of rock in the foreground framed it, and, as it shimmered in the light of the plain, it seemed to float above the land, insubstantial, unreal.

He frowned. Was he making too much of the crown of garrar feathers?

CHAPTER 3

The Temple of White Crystal

When he reached adolescence Bardek's pleas to be allowed to accompany Glidd to Bar-geda became so insistent that they knew they could not put it off any longer. If Glidd did not take him, he would go by himself.

And so it was agreed that the three of them should go together.

On the plains of Marvara they made camp twice. They stopped first for Glidd to show Bardek the honeycomb holes of the desert fagans, those small and cunning creatures who lived by stealing from the nests and stores of other animals. Glidd broke open one of their hideaways and revealed an extraordinary and intricate construction inside built from different shapes and sizes of spotlessly clean white bone, so delicate and fine that had it been larger the greatest architects would have been proud to have designed it. The floor was lined with feathers and fur for comfort.

The second time they stopped was beside a worked-out mirror-stone mine. The mineral had been taken and the land left scarred with pits, the residue a dull pink, and the bedrock, showing ribbed through the rubble, almost black. Glidd showed Bardek where he had once found a chip of mirror-stone left behind when the miners had departed, and while he and Firilla prepared food the boy searched, hoping to find a piece for himself. He had almost despaired of success when a silver glint caught his eye and he pulled aside a chunk of black rock to expose a small piece still attached to the ore. Excitedly he dug it out and rubbed it against his sleeve. It shone magnificently, and reflected in it he could see his face multiplied a dozen or more times. He stared at the images. 'Which one,' he thought, 'which one is the one that is the real me?' He had often felt as though he were a stranger – even to himself – as though he were acting out some other person's life.

'Bardek!' Firilla called. 'Bardek!'

Bardek? The name had been given him and for most of his life had contented him. He used to imagine meeting some-one on the mountain, someone not even Glidd knew about, who would ask who he was. 'Bardek,' he would reply. 'Bardek.' And the stranger would be satisfied. He had been given a name and he thought he now knew who Bardek was. But the name was only a device of convenience – if any-thing it prevented one looking for Oneself . . . or of truly seeing another . . .

No – not in the name lay the Self, but in the purpose for which a person was born. Bardek smashed the mirror-stone against a rock and kicked the myriad fragments of the face that mocked him . . . Why did he have these thoughts . . . Why? Glidd and Firilla did not question in this way. They lived their lives and were satisfied with eating and sleeping and loving each other and him. But for Bardek there was always something more . . . just out of reach . . . something he had to do . . . someone he had to be . . .

As they drew nearer the city Firilla became more and more uneasy. She had grown used to the quiet and the solitude of the mountains and feared to face crowds again. She looked anxiously at Bardek, wondering what effect the new environment and the new experiences would have on him.

Bar-geda was set in a spider shaped valley, the body of it closely packed with tall buildings and threaded with market streets, the limbs running away between the seven hills that dominated the periphery. Of these seven, three were natural and four were man-made. On six of them were strange and complex buildings, splendid and beautiful, but on the seventh was nothing but an immensely tall obelisk of black obsidian.

The most magnificent building of them all was the one on the highest natural hill. It was perched precariously on one side over a precipice and rose as though part of the rock itself, its tall white crystal walls fluting upwards to the sky in gleaming towers of needle like slenderness. Sometimes, as light caught the different facets, colours flashed and sparkled over the city like light ripples on water. This was the Temple of the White Star, the Star of mystics, clairvoyants and poets.

The second most impressive building, also on a natural hill, was the Blue Temple with its rounded domes in a countless array of sizes. This was Firilla's favourite and, after the Temple of the White Star, the one most respected by the community. Its domes were of translucent blue, casting brilliant and flickering webs of blue light over everything near it. Within its glowing depths the priestesses could sometimes be seen looking like water creatures swimming in a blue pool. Children born at the time of the Blue Star's greatest influence had a good chance of becoming priests or philosophers. Firilla had never ceased to remember that this should have been Bardek's Star.

Glidd's temple, the one serving the Red Star, the Star of the governors, the guardians and the hunters, was on one of the artificial mounds and was altogether smaller, a series of red cubes arranged in a very orderly way, one upon the other, the stone opaque.

The Green, the farmer's temple, was almost hidden amongst tall trenoids, its walls covered in a delicate lace of tendrils. The Indigo, in glass and metal, looked like a great feathered whain about to rise for flight; its legs tall metal columns holding the raised body above the flat-topped mound; its wings, shaped disks of shining metal, spread out on either side; its body every shade of purple, lavender, blue or indigo glass. Artists and musicians were its special charge. The rectangular yellow temple on the fourth man-made mound was for those who were happier working with their hands than their creative imaginations, for those who preferred to follow others than to make decisions for themselves.

The final hill, the last of the natural ones, was the one with no temple at all, only the obelisk of black glass from the fiery heart of a volcano rising like a sword of black light to pierce the sky. In a sense it served as a kind of time-dial, its ominous shadow marking the turn of the heavens above the city, constantly reminding the people who passed under it that the Dark Lord was always there, and that his time would come.

Firilla and Glidd had chosen to bring Bardek to Bar-geda at the time of the Festival of the White Star, feeling that this would be safest for the boy, with the influence of the Star of his conception at its strongest and that of his actual birth its weakest. Firilla had never been to the capital city before and clung to Glidd's hand so tightly she almost stopped the flow of blood to his fingers, but eventually, in spite of her fears for Bardek, she began to relax and respond to the excitement and joy of the celebration. Bardek was full of wonder, taking in everything that presented itself; the tall buildings, the narrow streets, the stall holders calling out their wares, the crowds dressed elaborately in their caste clothes, some with decorative emblems to mark the specific nature of their official role in society.

Ribbons of white paper were strung from roof to roof, window boxes of white flowers were scenting the air, and trailing vines of the white-leafed jabasco plant were gracefully hanging from many of them almost to ground level.

Glidd watched Bardek closely and scarcely noticed the crowds that pressed past them in the narrow streets. To his surprise the boy asked no questions, though everything he saw must have been full of mystery for him. He wondered if the people Bardek now encountered in the flesh were at all like the ones he had spoken to in 'imagination'.

Once deep in the city the hills with their extraordinary temple diadems were hardly visible. Only occasionally, rounding a corner, a flash of crystal light startled them, but was soon lost as their progress took them further under the overhang of balconies and into arcades and courtyards.

It was in a courtyard that they came to rest at last, sitting on a slab of veined and beautiful stone edging a fountain. It was an oasis of quiet in a desert of sound. Beside them the falling water hushed softly, exotic flowers in carved pots grew quietly. The noises of the city drew back, and waited, just beyond the range of their conscious attention.

'What do you think of it?' Glidd asked smiling, feeling a kind of pride and excitement in the city, as though it were his own and he were giving it as a gift to his friend.

Bardek's eyes glowed. 'It's wonderful!' he cried. 'What I would not give to live here forever!'

'No,' his mother said sharply. 'We have no place here.'

'Why not?' Bardek asked eagerly. 'There are shelters enough for a thousand mountain people.'

'You don't understand. This is not our place.'

Glidd noticed the growing sullen shadow in Bardek's eyes and was quick to change the subject. 'I'm hungry,' he said briskly, standing up and stretching. 'What do you say to a meal, my friends?' He could see the beginning of tears in Firilla's eyes and took her arm, turning her away from her son. 'A meal we don't have to cook on our own fire,' he added, 'and meat we've not hunted.' Bardek relaxed and smiled; he had not noticed how hungry he was until food was mentioned. 'And then we must find a place to sleep,' Glidd said.

Glidd led them through the streets he knew to an inn where the food was good, and Firilla joyously ordered valley fruit and leaf salad to make up for all the years that she had been living on a sparse mountain diet. This time it was nostalgia that nearly brought tears to her eyes, and she spoke long-ingly of the village and the fields she had once known. Glidd had brought her seeds and she had grown many things in her mountain home that did not normally grow there, but most needed the rich loam of the river plains and had sent up shoots in the mountains only to wilt and die.

'Try this!' she cried. 'And this!' She piled her son's bowl high with many amazing things, until he had to demand that she stop.

'Even I can't eat as much as that!' he laughed.

Glidd was happy to see that conflict had been averted, and called for wine. The boy's cheeks were flushed already with the food and the pleasure of being in the city, but the wine was silver and cool, light as water from an ice-melt in the mountains.

The inn had a room for them and after the meal Firilla insisted that they lie down and sleep, thinking that perhaps the sooner they were refreshed the sooner they could set off for their quiet home again. But Bardek lay awake, biding his time, knowing that only when they were asleep would he be free to explore the city on his own. He felt that he had invisible wings itching to be used and he would go mad if he were not allowed to stretch them soon.

He shut his eyes and flung his arm out over the side of the bed trying to convince the others he was asleep. It must have worked because he could no longer feel Glidd's eyes upon him, and when he ventured to open his own and lift his head, the man was sleeping, Firilla curled round on her side with her head on his shoulder and his cheek resting on her hair.

When Bardek was sure of their steady breathing, he rose quietly and left the room, glad to be free of the oppressive curtained darkness. The Temple of the White Star, palace of crystal on the highest hill, fascinated him, and he was determined to have a closer look at it.

He walked purposefully through the streets he had earlier wandered along so slowly, and followed every gleam and glint of white crystal he caught through the gaps in the buildings. But it was not as easy to find as he had thought. There seemed to be no logic to the streets and they changed direction frequently for no apparent reason. More often than not he found himself in a cul-de-sac and had to retrace his steps as though the city were a labyrinth designed to prevent him reaching the White Temple. He walked until he was weary and yet still seemed to be no nearer the outskirts of the city where he knew the white hill to be.

At first he was too shy to ask his way of the busy towns-people, but at last he stopped a boy and stammered out his question. He was given complicated instructions, which, after many left turns and right turns, led him back to where he had been before. Disheartened, he almost decided to turn back. It was taking longer than he had anticipated, and he was worried about his mother waking and finding him gone. But would he find his way back?

A woman holding a small child by the hand came hurrying round the corner. Bardek decided to make one more attempt. To have come so far without seeing the White Temple would be unendurable. 'I . . . I have lost my way. I wonder if you could . . .'

The woman was impatient, but she told him where to go. He fancied she looked at him strangely while he spoke, and at one point he thought she was going to warn him about something but thought better of it. After she left Bardek began to notice that the streets were emptying, the people seemed to be hurrying to find cover as though they knew something he did not. As he walked he searched his memory for all that Firilla had told him about the Star system. He could only remember being told good things about the White Star and its Temple. 'Of all the Stars that rule our planet,' she had said, 'the two most honoured are the White and the Blue. Those conceived and born under their influence are very fortunate.' When he had asked under which Star he had been born his mother had burst into tears and it had been Glidd who had answered for her.

'You were conceived under the Green, but you were born under the . . . Red.'

'The Star of bowmen, of guardians, of governors?'

Glidd had nodded briefly and turned away. 'Your Star, Glidd?'

'Yes.'

'Why does she weep?'

'She loves you. She weeps for the dangers bowmen and guardians have to face.'

'Why should I be a bowman or guardian? I could be a governor.' He knew the casting of horoscopes was more complicated than ordinary people believed, and within the period of a Star's influence there were many variations only Astrologers could trace.

Glidd had ignored his remark. 'When you are grown I will take you to my old lodge and you will become a hunter-bowman, and provide food for the villages of the dry lands where the burrars can't graze.'

'I will not leave my mother,' he had said then, fiercely, loyally. 'I will care for her until she is dead.' But he had been very young when he said that, and now, although he loved her still, he found her gentle tyranny irksome, and here he was upon an unknown road in an unknown city seeking . . . he knew not what.

As he turned a corner he staggered suddenly, as though he had been hit in the face.

He shut his eyes instinctively and covered them with his hands as a light that was stronger than he could have imagined beamed into them. Scarcely aware that he had moved he found himself crouching against a wall with his head buried in his arm, but even through the layers of flesh and bone he could feel the probing of the light.

'How can people endure it?' he thought, and then remembered the emptying of the streets, and that every house had its blinds down. He was torn between a strong desire to go back and an even stronger determination to go forward. 'The influence of the White Star is good,' Firilla had taught him time and again. 'Under its light are born the Seers, the mystics, those who are as far beyond us in wisdom as we are beyond the little six-legged fear-alls that hide under the rocks.'

Why should the light now drive fear into his heart? No

shadow could feel more menacing, nor darkness more sinister.

'I'll open my eyes and face it!'

Bardek felt challenged. Was it a weakness in himself that he could not look at it?

In the mountains the time of the White Star was bright, but never as bright as this. He remembered how when its rising was due the three of them invariably gathered to watch, and more often than not he had found tears in his eyes from the sheer beauty of it as it rose above the horizon. For a long time before its rising a pale silver flush mingled with the dim golden light of the Yellow Star's setting. Then there was a brilliant silver rim, brighter than mirror-stone, that shone along the whole length of the horizon. Suddenly one part of it grew thicker, brighter. They held their breath. Then an overwhelming splendour burst into a million dazzling beams that sparked from cliff face and summit.

It was true that when it was fully risen he could not look at it directly, but the light of it that touched everything into sparkle and shine was good, and he had never feared it before.

'The White Star is the only one we can't look at directly,' he thought now. 'But surely the Star itself can't be closer in the city than it is in the mountains?'

He eased his arm gradually from his face, but felt impelled to keep his eyes still tightly closed. Was it his imagination or was the light less strong already?

He waited, eyes closed, having the strange sensation that where his eyes normally were there were now two deep pits, not dark as pits should be, but filled with a swirling interplay of lights of every colour. He seemed to be looking inwards rather than outwards, and found himself straining to see into the pits of light as though he expected something to emerge from them.

Suddenly he cried out as the light seemed to stop swirling for a moment and a hint, a flash of something, appeared to him. What was it? A shape . . . a figure . . . a figure reaching out to him . . .

Desperate to see more clearly and impatient with the indistinctness of the vision, he opened his eyes.

He found himself looking directly at the Temple of the White Star, his eyes smarting and watering with the strain of looking at so strong a source of light. He kept blinking them and straining them to stay open for longer and longer periods of time until at last he could see the temple without too much discomfort. It was still a distance from him, but he could see it full and clear, crowning the hill, catching the light of the Star, focusing it and reflecting it, magnified across the land. It was built of crystal, a cluster of tall forms, each reflecting surface catching the light at different moments.

Bardek began to notice that the pain in his eyes was growing less. He wiped them with his sleeve, and looked again with amazement at the building. Tower upon tower of transparent crystal sparkled against the sky while occasionally lights of other colours glinted for an instant and were gone. He had never dreamed of such beauty. He moved forward. To reach the Temple and bathe in its light had become the most important and urgent thing in his life. He left the town behind and started to climb the steep hill. At first it was easy, but he soon found that he had to pause for breath. The trenoids that clustered around the hill frequently hid the Temple's crystal towers, their spiralling tendrils and the shimmering splendour of their variegated leaves forming a colourful curtain between him and the object of his quest.

He looked back at the town and saw that the streets were no longer empty. The unendurable brilliance had left them and the people who had chosen to draw their blinds and sleep through the experience were awake and busy with their affairs. Bardek smiled slightly, recalling that while Firilla was afraid of the dark here it seemed they were afraid of the light. He did not blame them, for he was still shaken from his own encounter with it.

He thought about Glidd and Firilla and felt again the pressure of time upon him. But he had come too far now and he was determined not to return to them until he had explored the temple. He tried to shut his mind to the worry he knew Firilla would be feeling if she had noticed that he was missing.

He moved forward and upward.

As he reached higher up the hill the way became steeper and steeper, and he found himself sometimes on his knees, reaching for the exposed fibrous roots and the scaly trunks of the saplings, testing them before he put his weight on them, using them to haul himself up. There seemed to be no path, but certain places were more open than others. He wondered if just around the other side of the hill there were not steps, or even a road, leading to the Temple, but if there were it would probably be guarded. He preferred to stay where he was and avoid being seen.

Suddenly he was at the top.

The trenoids and their undergrowth had hidden the fact that he was so near, and his surprise as he stood upon flat ground and stared at the open and magnificent scene before him took his breath away.

The Temple was surrounded by gardens of flowers and by fountains. Every kind of white flower he had ever known and many that he had never dreamed of budded and bloomed, all poised on perfection as though there were no tomorrow of falling petals and browning leaves. Tall showers of water caught the light and sparked with a myriad fleeting colours. He could see the Temple through the veil of drops, its gleaming crystal almost indistinguishable from the water. Cautiously he looked around to see if there were any guardians to challenge him, but the place seemed deserted. He took one step, then another. At last he strode boldly forward. As he reached the line of fountains he could feel the cool prickle of the water drops on his skin. He shivered with pleasure. The struggle up the hill had made him sweat uncomfortably; dust and broken pieces of bark-scale had clung to him and made him feel dirty and sticky. The cool spray washed over him and he emerged at last through its fine veil refreshed and invigorated.

Beyond the fountains there was nothing between him and the transparent walls of the Temple. Curiosity drove him on but the knowledge that he was trespassing in a sacred place made him advance with the caution of a hunter.

He stopped within a few paces of the walls and found that he was looking into a great hall, all the inner walls of which were as transparent as the outer ones. Beyond it he could see passages and chambers disappearing into the distance. The immediate hall was completely bare save for a tall plinth of white marble at the centre of which was a gigantic skull carved out of rock crystal. The floor in particular caught his attention: an intricate geometric design, each piece of stone a different shade of white, each complex arrangement of crystal slab leading the eye back to the centre, back to the skull. The front of the skull's face, where the eye and nose sockets were, was of totally clear crystal, blank and empty, but in the cranium fine cracks in the rock gave the impression of floating filaments of shimmering mystery. He thought of the sky on a deep dark night, the time of the Dark Star, when there was no great source of light, only those floating filaments of distant shining mist and minute specks and points of brightness. It seemed to him that in looking into the domed skull he was looking into the mighty universe beyond their small planet, and had a strange cold moment of wonder whether in fact the universe was contained in man, or man in the universe.

Before he had time to follow this thought through, he noticed a movement deep in the building. He had thought at first that the whole place was deserted, but now he could see, faintly at first, but growing clearer all the time, a procession of people coming towards the hall he was watching, down a long, long corridor. They came slowly, and it was some time before he could make out the details of the procession, but he knew they must be priests. By the measured order of their progress he was sure also that they were engaged in ritual. A fine, clear chanting was in the air as much outside as inside the building. Bardek looked quickly round for shelter. He wanted to see what was going to happen more than he had ever wanted anything in his life, but he did not want to be seen. If he retreated beyond the veil of the fountains, he would not be able to see what was going on in the hall. He decided to lie flat on the cold white paving stones behind a bed of tall lilies and take a chance that he would not be noticed.

The chanting stopped and he raised his head in alarm. Had he been discovered? But he had no need to worry; the chanting had stopped because the procession had reached its destination. The figures of the priests were grouped in a wide circle around the skull, their eyes closed and their heads tilted slightly as though listening to something he could not hear.

After a long time the silence and the stillness became unbearable. Bardek, cramped and uncomfortable on the hard stone, his limbs itching to move, began to wonder if he should get up and creep away while the priests eyes were closed, but then he noticed that someone else was entering the hall and curiosity made him forget his discomfort.

A tall priest led the way, followed by three figures. Forgetting his vulnerability, Bardek began to creep forward, straining to see more clearly. They were certainly not moving with the measured tread of the first group. The tall one in front, dressed in stiff folds of gleaming white, a crown of crystal on his head, necklaces of silver and diamond hanging from his shoulders almost to his waist, was presumably the High Priest. He began to lead his little group in what was at first a wide arc around the still and silent priests, narrowing on each turn to join the circle already in position. Bardek gasped: the two outer figures were holding a third between them, and the third was struggling to escape.

'Surely,' he thought with horror, 'I'm not going to witness a sacrifice!' He had heard that in ancient times under the Dark Lord there had been sacrifices – but in these times, and in such a place? Hardly breathing now, he forgot caution and crept nearer the crystal wall to see and hear more clearly.

The tall priest came almost face to face with him, and it seemed to Bardek that his heart jerked sickeningly. Now he was surely finished, the man had looked straight at him! But it seemed he had not been seen. Bardek could not believe it; the eyes of all the priests were open now and many must surely have noticed him, but not one showed any sign that he had. Was it possible that the light of the White Star and the nature of the crystal combined in such a way that those inside could not see out?

Bardek thought for a while, then stood up and peered boldly through the wall. As the moments passed and he was still not discovered he began to forget his own danger and concentrate on the scene before him.

The three figures behind the High Priest had now come clearly into view and were breaking into the circle of priests to be nearer the central plinth and crystal skull. The men were drawing back to let them pass.

As the prisoner struggled, the cloak that had hidden his features fell away and Bardek was startled to find himself looking at a girl no older than himself.

For a moment, with the falling of the cloak, she managed to break away from her captors and run to the outer wall, beating at it with her clenched hands, a few inches of crystal all that separated her from him. He could see into her eyes and was overwhelmed with pity for the desperation in them. At that moment he decided he would do everything he could to help her escape.

He started beating with his own fists on the wall, shouting blasphemies at the priests for holding such a young girl captive. To his surprise the sound his fists made seemed to have penetrated to the hall, because the circle broke up in confusion, and the whole throng crowded to the wall, peering myopically, trying to see who was causing the disturbance on the outside. Even the girl was startled, and instead of taking the chance of the diversion to escape stood foolishly staring at the wall.

Now that he was certain they could not see out of the

Temple, Bardek felt extremely bold and shouted abuse and demanded that they release her. For a moment he fancied they might obey him, they were so surprised by his intrusion, but the moment passed and the priest who seemed to be in charge raised his arm and commanded them back to their places. They obeyed instantly, and the girl was seized, and vanished from his sight within the circle of men, her cloak still lying on the magnificent floor.

In spite of the fact that he had heard nothing but good about the Temple of the White Star, the girl's feelings of terror and longing for escape so communicated themselves to Bardek that he was convinced she was about to be sacrificed. He ran around the building searching for a door, but the bland crystal seemed endless, stretching up almost as far as he could see, and on no surface could he find a break of any kind. The whole Temple appeared completely sealed within itself.

Whenever he saw someone moving within the chambers he passed he beat on the wall and called, but no one saw him. Some looked up, momentarily puzzled, but soon went back to what they were doing and ignored the intrusion.

Surely there was a door . . . a window . . . an air vent of some kind? There must be some way of moving from the outside to the inside. But if there was, Bardek could not find it.

Frantic and frustrated, he found himself at last back where he had started, at the Hall of the Skull. He stood helplessly with his arms against the wall, peering in, expecting to see the girl's body dismembered and bleeding on the floor. Instead he saw her standing tall and proud, her arms lifted above her head, her voice ringing with strength and power, the priests kneeling before her, their heads lowered in respect. He was so amazed at the sight he did not hear what she was saying. A great feeling of desolation came upon him. He understood nothing. The girl was elated, powerful, triumphant. Had he imagined her eyes full of fear and despair? He stood for a while staring at the scene and then, filled with weariness and a sense of anti-climax, he turned and plodded back through the falling water and the white flowers to the trenoids that rimmed the hill. Slithering and sliding he was soon down to the valley, only a few scratches and a tear in his breeches to show for his adventure.

The way back to the Inn seemed longer than he remembered, but he did not once think about the direction. Some skill below the level of consciousness guided him back to where Firilla was weeping and Glidd was tight-lipped and angry. He would not tell them where he had been or what he had witnessed, but when they said that they were going straight home to the mountains he agreed eagerly, not even asking for a rest before the journey.

Firilla and Glidd looked at each other, surprised, but they asked no questions.

Bardek's eyes almost filled with tears when he at last saw the wooden house nesting against the rock with his mother's varied and colourful flowers surrounding it. Home! He was glad to draw its familiar cloak around him . . .

CHAPTER 4

The Garrar Fight

For a long while after this Bardek was reasonably content with his life in the mountains. He found as he grew older that there was still a great deal to learn, not only about the bowman's craft, but about nature. More and more he would go off by himself, spending a great deal of time observing the creatures of the wild, tracking, studying, thinking.

Glidd spoke of taking him to his old Hunter's Lodge that lay to the south in the foothills. 'I've taught you all I know and it's time for you to meet others of our caste. You are good with the bow, but you will find many who are better. The competition will be good for you.'

He told Bardek of the tournaments that were held, when bowmen from all over the mountains and the plains gathered at one or other of the lodges to compete against each other. His eyes shone when he thought of the time when he, on the verge of manhood, no older than Bardek now was, had won the coveted trophy.

Firilla was against it and needed some persuading, but at last she gave in and agreed that Bardek could go if Glidd promised to stay with him.

Just before they were due to go, Bardek returned to the place that had been his favourite as a child, the natural amphitheatre of rock from which he could, on a clear day, see the distant smudge on the horizon that was Bar-geda, framed between two great columns of rock.

He sat on the flat rock he had so often used as a platform for his orations when he was younger. He thought of Glidd and how agitated he had been to find him crowned with garrar feathers. He wondered if the crown was still where he had hidden it from Glidd. It was so long since he had looked at it that small rock plants had grown over the boulder that served as a door. He had to scratch them away before he could pull it out and feel in the cavity behind. The crown was still there, somewhat bedraggled. The black feathers that had once shone and flashed with red light were dull and shabby. He turned it round and round in his hands, sad that time had robbed it of its glamour. It even seemed smaller than he remembered, and when he lifted it to his head to try and recapture something of the pleasure he had had at his first crowning, it did not fit.

He sighed.

His thoughts drifted back to Bar-geda and his experiences there. When he first returned to the mountains he had deliberately busied himself so that he would not think about the disturbing events at the Temple. As time passed, the memories had become so faded they no longer presented a threat to his peace of mind. But now, sitting alone on the mountain, in this particular place where so many strange thoughts had come to him in the past, knowing that he was on the verge of another great change, his thoughts went back to the girl.

He frowned. The memory of her was vivid, almost as though he were in her presence again. He found himself remembering things about her that he had not realised he had noticed before. Her beauty was astounding. No one he had ever seen or dreamed of could compare with her. Her eyes haunted him, deeply grey-green with golden flecks, the lashes even longer than Firilla's. Her hair was silver – not white as he had seen the hair of very old people, but pure silver like the light of the White Star itself. Her body was perfect and there were things about it that had passed him by before which now tormented him. He longed to see her again, to take her out of the Temple, to be with her.

In imagination he walked around the Temple again,

searching for an entrance or an opening of some kind. He could not believe that there were none. Was he the victim of an illusion?

He stood up suddenly, determined to return to the city and the Temple and make one more attempt to reach her. Glidd and his Lodge would have to wait.

The procession of Stars had passed many times since he was first at Bar-geda, and it was the time of the White Star again, but past its zenith and well on the way to setting. He wondered what happened to the White Temple when its special Star had set. Did it grow dull and lifeless? Was it then possible for the people inside to see out through the walls? Would the ritual still continue and the mysterious frail prisoner be led in, weeping, only to transform into a powerful Being in front of the crystal skull?

Bardek knew that if he had to face Firilla or Glidd now his resolution would waver. He decided to go straight to the city. He took off the crown of garrar feathers and plucked one out from the others, using the quill of it to write a message for Glidd on a flat pad of compacted soil. He marked the place with his red bowman's scarf, weighting it with small pieces of rock, the crown lying discarded and forgotten beside it. He stayed only to gather a pouch full of mountain roots and berries he knew were good and nourishing to eat and to fill his water bottle.

Firilla and Glidd did not miss Bardek until the time for sleep, and even then they saw no cause to worry. He had seemed content for a long time now and often spent time alone in the mountains.

But when they had been asleep for some time Firilla was woken by a storm. The lightning seemed to tear the sky apart, and the thunder to shake the mountain rocks until they rattled. Firilla turned closer into the arms of her lover and would have slept in spite of the noise had she not remembered Bardek. She looked to his bed; it was empty.

'Glidd!' she cried, shaking him awake.

Half dazed he saw her white face staring at him in the sudden illumination of a flash of lightning.

'What is it?'

'Bardek. He's still not back!'

Glidd groaned and rolled over on his elbow to view Bardek's sleeping corner. 'The Dark Lord take him!' he cursed under his breath.

Firilla heard him and looked horrified, tears springing to her eyes. 'Why do you say that? Are you mad?'

Glidd, now fully awake, was contrite. 'I didn't mean it love; no harm will come to him.'

'Pray to the Lord of Light, the White Star itself, before your evil message leaves this room,' she cried, her face pinched with anxiety.

Glidd made the sign of the White Star and said the prayer she wanted, but it did not seem to comfort her. She was still trembling, her eyes dark with distress.

'You'll not come to my bed until my son returns safe,' she burst out, sobbing. He looked at her with amazement. 'You have cursed him and exposed him to evil. If he falls under it, I'll never forgive you.'

He had never known her so bitter, so vindictive. 'Firilla!' He tried to put his arms round her but she drew back.

'No. Not until he is safe.'

'This is nonsense. I didn't really curse him. It was an idle phrase people use all the time. It means nothing!'

'It means a great deal.'

The house shook with a gigantic clap of thunder and, forgetting her vow, she screamed and clung to Glidd. For a moment he thought that he was reprieved, but his relief was short lived. As soon as the sound grumbled off into the distance she sprang away from him and drew the bed clothes up round her, looking at him fiercely over the top of her drawn up knees.

'I'll go and look for him if it'll make you happier,' he said. 'But you'll see – no harm will have come to him.'

She did not answer, but stared at him with dark eyes, watching as he stood up and put on his clothes, watching as he walked to the door. Before he left he looked back, hoping to see a change in her expression. But there was none, and he knew that she had meant her threat.

The thunder and lightning had spent itself now and heavy rain fell like a waterfall upon the house. He looked ruefully at it. It was madness to go out and look for Bardek. The boy would have had the sense to get under cover at the first sign of the storm and would return when it was over. But Firilla was in no mood to be told this, so he walked out into the violent downpour, thinking of some harsh things to say to Bardek when he found him.

Miserably he trudged away from the house and within moments was drenched. He ducked under a ledge and sat crouched and brooding for a while, thinking of his bed, sure that it would not be long before he would be back beside Firilla.

But when the rain abated and some time had passed and there was still no sign of Bardek, Glidd set off to look for him, an instinct telling him to go to the amphitheatre of rock where he had found him once before. The way was long, and with the rock and soil so wet, dangerous. 'He is probably home already,' thought Glidd bitterly, but there was enough unease in his mind for him to check the amphitheatre before he gave up. He prayed that he would find the boy there, for he did not look forward to returning without Firilla's son.

Water was running wild. The wet walls of rock gleamed with it. Cracks rushed with it. Muddy pools were collecting everywhere. Glidd slipped and slithered on the track, nearly falling to his death several times.

The air had a great clarity now and although the White Star was near its setting and the light dimmer than it had been, the colours of the mountains and the plains were brighter, clearer, sharper, than they usually were, tinged with indigo and purple. He was confident that he would find

Bardek whistling along the path to meet him at any moment. He whistled himself a while, the light clean air lifting his heart in spite of what had just happened with Firilla.

He reached the amphitheatre of rock and found it scoured clean by the recent storm. Bardek was not there.

Glidd called long and loud, using the echoes to carry his voice round the mountain further than it would normally have reached, but no answer came back to him. Only his own voice, mocking.

Caught on a low shrub he found the bedraggled and broken crown of garrar feathers, and further down the ravine where water from the amphitheatre had spilled violently over, he saw the gleam of something red. The rain had washed Bardek's message away, but his scarf was found by a horrified Glidd, soaked and muddy at the bottom of a steep drop of rock.

Trembling with the fear of what he might find, Glidd lowered himself down the dangerous cliff, pausing every now and then to call the boy. His heart ached, his fingers bled as he tore them on the rocks, the curse he had spoken without thinking returning to haunt him. Would all the prayers in the world to the Lord of the White Star cancel out that careless phrase, spoken half asleep?

Firilla's eyes seemed to be everywhere, accusing him. How could he return to her with the bones of her son and say honestly that he had no part in killing him?

He reached the scarf at last and used it to bind his knee, which had received a severe jarring on a rock. There was no sign of anything else of the boy's, but the ravine went further. Glidd struggled on in despair, his mind in conflict, one part of it refusing to believe that this was actually happening, the other seeing images of the boy's broken and bleeding body at every turn.

The thought crossed his mind that he would not return to face Firilla, but he loved her too much to do that to her. Whether she took him to her bed or not, she would need help from him if Bardek was dead. She might never forgive him, but she would need him.

The crown of garrar feathers kept coming to his mind and he wondered what part the Dark Lord had played in Bardek's disappearance. Surely it was no coincidence that the boy's fall to death was from the place where he had found the crown?

He searched long and thoroughly, but he found no more trace of Bardek. At last, wearily, he struggled back up the mountain and returned to Firilla.

She was waiting for him away from the house, standing on an upthrust rock, her feet planted well apart as though she had been standing there for some time, scanning for her lover and her son. When she saw Glidd returning alone, his clothes torn and muddied, his face tired and drawn, her own face tightened and the eyes that questioned him were as cold as rock.

'Isn't he home, yet?' Glidd asked, knowing by her expression that he was not.

She said nothing, but looked at him with terrible eyes and then she turned from him and ran back to the house, going straight inside and shutting the door.

'Firilla!' he called, his heart aching with sympathy for her. Exhausted as he was, he forced himself the last few paces to the house and put his hand to the door. It was not locked. 'Firilla,' he said gently, 'I didn't find him dead.'

But she would not look at him.

'Firilla, he will be back soon. I'm sure of it.'

But still she did not speak or turn to him. It was as though the woman he had known so long and loved so well had left, and only the shell of her body remained.

The mountain that had been so full of noise when the storm raged was deathly silent now. For some reason even the whains were still and the shuttered house was the most silent place of all.

Glidd turned sadly away and went outside. The storm had flattened Firilla's garden, and where tall stems had supported proud and beautiful flowers, where leaves and berries had flourished green and purple, all was broken, limp, sad, like the heart of the woman who had called them from the rocky soil and cherished them so tenderly to life.

On his journey, Bardek had seen the black clouds lowering over the mountains, felt the ominous oppression of their weight upon his back, and when the storm broke he found a place to rest and eat where he could watch the display of light and dark doing battle on the distant peaks.

He wondered about Firilla and Glidd and felt regret that he would worry them, sorrow that he had to leave them, but his obsession with the girl was stronger than regret or sorrow. Was it desire that drove him on? Did he want the girl with the silver hair as Glidd wanted Firilla and, if so, what difficulties would he have to face to win her as his woman?

The storm itself did not reach him, but the effect of it did. He was resting in a dry, quiet gully when a roaring, rushing, grinding sound reached him. Puzzled, he sat still for a while trying to place it amongst the sounds he knew. When he could not he climbed the gully wall to get a better view of the land in the direction from which it was coming.

It was this that saved his life, for within moments of his leaving it the gully became a seething, roaring mass of turbulent water, the force of it carrying great boulders before it, which would surely have destroyed him if the water had not.

Bardek was astonished and shaken. He knew that storms brought sudden streams and waterfalls to life in the mountains, but he had seen nothing like this. Malevolently the brown and frothing mass hurled itself at the banks of the gully, breaking off great chunks of the walls, the rock and soil and twisted debris adding to the volume every moment. The noise was deafening and he was suddenly separated from the path he had intended to take by an impassable and violent river. He moved back hastily, fearing the undercutting of the banks as the water hurtled against them. The whole landscape around him was changing. The plain, which must have been honeycombed with dried, underground watercourses, was now becoming pitted with caverns as the fragile roofs of rock above them collapsed. Bardek could see that he would have to change his path, but he did not once consider returning home.

Picking his way carefully, he walked along the bank, hoping to find a convenient place to cross, not realising how subtly the river was altering direction and how irrevocably he was being led away from his destination.

At last he was too weary to continue. He told himself that the river which had started so suddenly must surely disappear as suddenly. As he could not find its end, he would wait for it to pass. He found a bush with a twisted trunk and sat propped against it, preparing for a long wait. The light changed subtly, exquisitely, each rocky outcrop passing through a complicated range of tones, the scene before him not the same from one moment to the next. How far away the horizon was in this flat place! How every detail loomed in his attention and then faded as the last rays of the White Star picked out a different object to illumine, one moment the angular lines of a rock, the next the soft curves of sandfall and wind-flower.

He looked at the mountains in the distance, his mountains, and saw how insubstantial they appeared, each range behind the other glowing through as though transparent. His eyes grew heavy, the music of the water sounds around him lulling him, soothing him, sleep falling on him like a soft dark cloak.

He heard what was at first a slight note of change in the sounds of the desert, which wove into his dream as though it were part of it . . . but then it became so insistent, so loud, he could not ignore it. He woke in time to see the ground around him collapse and to feel the harsh buffeting of the flood that carried him away. As he lost consciousness in its icy grip he remembered that he had heard of underground rivers whose black water had never seen the light, nor nourished plant or quenched the thirst of man. Was it into one of these that he was falling?

When he regained consciousness the river had disappeared, but so had the desert plains and the mountains and the distant city. He sat up, startled. He was in darkness, but it was not the darkness of the Dark Star. It was the darkness of a windowless chamber.

He peered around, straining to catch the outline of some familiar object, half hoping that Glidd had found him and carried him safely home, yet disappointed if this was the case that his adventure was over so soon. Becoming aware of a sliver of light to one side, he stood up shakily, wincing as he moved, every part of him aching and stinging, his head throbbing. His clothes were torn and caked with dried mud, and he could feel that blood had congealed beside his left eye. He felt along a rough wall of reeds and straw until he reached the crack of light. It was, as he had hoped, a door. It gave easily to his push, revealing an astonishing and bewildering scene. The light was dim, the White Star almost set, the Indigo not yet fully risen. He could see that he was surrounded by huts similar to the one he was in, dank hovels made of blackened reeds, each held high above the surface of dark and stagnant water by tall stilts, a low mist slithering between them. Here and there islands of floating detritus gave off a noxious smell.

That he had been washed away from the plain and all that was familiar to him was clear, but how he came to be in a house in a village in the marshlands was not so clear. Someone must have found him and brought him here, and yet there seemed to be nobody about.

Marshlands! He started. Glidd had once told him of people he called 'the marsh-dwellers', people of the Dark Star, misfits and criminals, hopeless savages, wild and cruel robbers and murderers. His heart beat uncomfortably. What was to be done? Perhaps it would be possible to leave before anyone returned. He noted with dismay the long drop to the water: the ladder that gave access to most of the other huts was missing from the one he was in.

Suddenly there was a sound from the left and he turned

his head in time to see a small flat punt emerging from behind one of the houses, propelled by a youth of about his
own age, crudely and raggedly clad, hair dirty and matted.
Bardek stood back in the shadows watching, not sure if he
wanted to be noticed or not. He was just deciding to risk
asking a question or two when a loud noise above the houses
distracted him. It was a terrible sound, the wild screech howl
of the garrar. Bardek had heard it sometimes in the mountains, but always from a distance, and even then it had made
him shudder.

It seemed near, as though it were just above the hut in
which he was standing, and so loud it was probable that there
was more than one of the fearsome beasts.

Bardek saw the youth in the craft look up in terror and
even as he feverishly worked the punt pole in an attempt to
slide under the cover of the houses one of the garrars
swooped, while its mate hovered shrieking in anticipation
of the coming meal. Bardek saw the youth beat ineffectually
at the creature with his pole, his face twisting in agony as
one of the great talons tore into the flesh of his shoulder.
Luckily for the youth the garrar's wingtip touched one of
the stilts of the hut and it momentarily lost purchase. In the
brief respite this afforded, the victim managed to get the tip
of his pole into the eye of the beast and it retreated with a
scream of pain, its wings flapping wildly.

So huge were the beasts and so violent the beating of
their wings that the sludgy marsh water was churned up
around the punt, even the houses rocking perilously in the
turbulence.

Bardek seized everything loose he could find within the
hut and hurled it out at the monsters, wishing desperately
that he had his bow or spear. He shouted and roared as he
threw, trying to create as much of a diversion as possible,
thinking that he was safe in the hut. But his missiles were no
more than slight irritants to the garrars and barely distracted
them from their cruel game.

If only he had fire!

Glidd had taught him that when he was holed up in a mountain cave far from home, and darkness brought the danger of beasts of prey, he was to make fire at the entrance to the cave and this would frighten off marauders. He remembered that he had fire powders in his breeches pocket and felt anxiously for them, afraid that either he had been robbed or that they would be too wet to use. But the powders were still there safe in their little flasks and dry enough. With trembling hands he mixed them in a bowl he found on the dirty, greasy floor, and when the flame at last had taken shape he rushed to the door. The youth was still alive, crouching in his frail craft under the overhang of one of the houses.

But the garrars had not given up. The one with the blinded eye was tearing and beating at the house above the boy with a kind of crazed vengefulness, while the other was making low flying swoops, trying to grab him as it passed. The youth had lost the pole and was desperately beating the air with his fists, blood pouring down his body from the wound in his shoulder.

Bardek ripped a piece of straw lining from the reed walls and set it alight. At first he waved it like a torch, but as this had no effect he flung it with all his might at one of the beasts. It missed and fell with a sharp spatter of sparks into the water, hissing as it touched, black and acrid smoke rising at once to join the dark and fearsome scene.

Bardek ripped and pulled at the walls of the hut, lighting bundles and hurling them, his throat and eyes smarting from the smell of mouldy burning straw. One bundle hit the wing of a garrar and caused it to veer and screech and miss its mark.

He was so excited at his success and so anxious to get the next fire stick on its way he upturned the bowl with his foot, and within seconds the whole hut was on fire. Horrified, he was caught between two possible deaths, each as painful as the other. The inside of the hut was rapidly becoming a furnace while outside the furious garrars were swooping and screeching.

He could not stay in the hut. That was certain. He leapt from the door. The fire death was a certainty, but with the garrars there might be a chance. As he hit the water he shut his eyes, taking a deep breath before he went under. He struggled with water weeds and old rotting logs, but eventually came to the surface.

As he shook the strands of reed and mud from his eyes he was shocked to see that he was almost surrounded by fire. The fire sticks he had thrown must have hit some of the other houses, for they, as well as the one he had been in, were in flames. He felt someone seize his arm and turned to find the youth he had been trying to help was now helping him. He was trying to haul him out of the water on to the punt.

Thankfully, he clutched the sides and clambered out. The garrars had been frightened off and fire was their enemy now. The two knew that their only chance was to work the water with their arms and try to pull away before the burning houses collapsed on top of them. The stranger could only use one arm, the other hanging loose from the garrar wound, but Bardek was strong and fear made him stronger. He paddled with all his might and mercifully the light craft responded. They slid out of reach just as the huts collapsed behind them. Showers of sparks rose to the sky and the water heaved and surged like an evil broth as the logs that had held the huts upright plunged into it. Their boat almost capsized, but somehow Bardek kept it the right way up and drove it further and further from the danger. When they were sure they were safe they stopped paddling and lay gasping in the punt like stranded water creatures.

Gradually, as their breath came more evenly, Bardek began to be aware of new sounds coming from the direction of the fire. There was still the awful crackling of the flame as it consumed the wooden houses, but now the sound of angry shouting mingled with it – a fleet of small boats was just discernible through the black smoke. The villagers were returning to find their homes nothing more than greasy ash floating on the scum and slime that already covered the water.

Bardek looked at his companion. He was looking back at the towering column of black smoke that rose from behind the high reeds. His face was turned away so that at first Bardek could not see his expression, but when he turned Bardek was startled by the fear in his eyes. There was no trace of sorrow.

'They are not your people? Your family?' he asked.

The boy shook his head vigorously and then the pain almost made him lose consciousness. Bardek reached forward and steadied him. What was to be done? If that wound was not attended to the youth might lose his arm, possibly his life. He looked at the water. It was not clean enough to wash the wound, yet the stranger was pleading with him to take him away, and seemed as afraid of the people in the boats as he had been of the garrar beasts. For the first time Bardek noticed a rag bundle in the bottom of the punt, fallen half open to reveal the gleam of precious metal. The village had been deserted; was his companion a thief? That such a collection of huts could contain anything worth stealing was a surprise, but Glidd had told him that the followers of the Dark Lord had elaborate rituals of worship just as they did for their own Holy Ones. Such rituals might well call for the use of precious artefacts.

'Where are your people?' It seemed the only hope would be to return the boy to the care of his own family.

The young marsh-dweller muttered something and then slid forward in a faint, almost into the water. Bardek caught him and held him up, trying to think. He could see that to go back to the burning village and ask the help of the villagers would be useless. But to go on through this weird, festering, watery place without knowing where he was going was dangerous. The marshlands, the water lands, were hostile places. He had been brought up to believe that they were the domain of the Lord of the Dark Star and that no good could come out of them.

While he considered the alternatives, Bardek pulled at the water and the reeds with his aching arms and moved the boat slowly, painfully, forward, away from the village. Gradually the smoke disappeared behind them, the sounds grew fainter until he could hear nothing but the slight slurp of the boat through the water. He had never seen such a flat place. Even the desert plain he had just crossed had gullies and rocky outcrops to vary the surface, but here the reeds rose above the water at a constant height and, beyond them, the sky seemed to go on forever.

After a while he found himself moving into mist and tried to turn round. But the reeds had closed in behind him and he could not manoeuvre the boat round. He thought longingly of Firilla and Glidd in their warm and comfortable house and began to shiver as the damp mist penetrated his clothes and fear of the unknown grew in his heart. The marshlands were uncannily quiet, and he felt increasingly that he was alone in a vast water world that had no end and no beginning, with a boy who was about to die. His former life seemed like a dream, the only reality the effort he was putting into his aching arms to pull at the sluggish water. The crowding reeds became each moment taller and thicker and more oppressive. At last he stopped working with his arms and moved back into the boat to crouch beside the boy, his head against his chest, anxiously listening for a heartbeat. The punt, which had been moving very slowly forward under the impetus of his last push, stopped with a jerk. Startled, he looked up. At first he could not make anything out, but then realised that the punt had come to rest against a causeway made of logs lashed together and piled one upon the other to raise it above the surface of the water. Joyfully he thought of what this could mean. People. Villages. Help.

He wedged the punt against one of the logs and started to haul the unconscious youth out of the boat. He was heavy and the craft rocked sickeningly with Bardek's clumsy attempts, but at last he had him in his arms and managed to lift him on to the wooden platform of the causeway. Unfortunately the effort he put into this destabilised the punt and it shot backwards, depositing him into the muddy water. He floundered at first, flailing uselessly with his tired arms, but at last managed to grip one of the protruding lower logs and haul himself out of the water.

The boy lay awkwardly where he had been left, while Bardek lay beside him, panting after his exertions. He was so tired he would have been content to rest there forever . . . but he began to shiver uncontrollably . . . soaking wet, with the eerie mist that was slinking from the surface of the marsh curling round them with cold and clammy tendrils. He forced himself to move, rubbing his own limbs to get the circulation going, and then those of his companion. The boy opened his eyes and groaned. Bardek at once leant closer and peered into his face, meeting the young man's eyes for an instant before he slid back into unconsciousness. Bardek could see that if they were to survive it would be up to him. He lifted the youth as best he could on to his shoulders and, staggering under the weight, set off along the causeway. The path was very narrow, with logs frequently missing. He had to watch his step. The mist was becoming thicker and more impenetrable and Bardek was very near to despair. Would he ever reach habitation, and even if he did, would it bring shelter – or death?

Suddenly, he thought he saw a glow through the mist off to the right. Treading cautiously, he established that the causeway branched at this point and that one of the branches led toward the light. The relief made him hurry and he lost his footing. With a thud he and his burden fell to the slippery path.

The light went out.

CHAPTER 5

A Question of Tribe

Firilla did not keep Glidd from her bed as she had said she would, and life continued, on the surface at least, with a semblance of calm. But Bardek's disappearance and Glidd's ill-advised curse hung over them always like a shadow. When Glidd came to bed he would invariably find Firilla already asleep, or more often feigning sleep. He lay beside her, desiring her but not touching her. As a hunter he knew how to wait patiently, and he knew now that he had to wait for Firilla's heart to come out of the dark covert of its pain before he could recapture it. He would make her see that it was not his apparent invocation of the Dark Lord that had destroyed her son, but a perfectly ordinary mountain storm that could have hit at any time.

He understood her fears, for there were times when he had been as superstitious as she was. But there were other times when he doubted the power of the rigid hierarchy of stars that were said to rule their lives. He would wait, he would continue his search for Bardek. But he believed him dead, and he would try to teach her how to live without her son. He was certain his own love would win through her stubborn bitterness in the end and she would turn to him again.

Staring into the darkness beside her, feeling her rigid and un-sleeping, he thought of how they used to make love and afterwards how she slept curled like a leaf, breathing softly.

* * * *

When Bardek regained consciousness, he and the youth were lying together on a low bed in a room with walls of reed similar to the one he had escaped from, but this time it was full of people. Instinctively he clenched his fists, for the faces leaning over him were hostile and rough. One in particular, who seemed to be the leader, had long and matted black hair and a bristling beard that was a mixture of red and grey. His eyes were wary and he fingered a knife as Bardek turned his face towards him. Bardek groaned inwardly – to come through all that they had done and then die at the hands of this man! He tried to raise himself, but there was no strength in his limbs. He fell helplessly back upon the bed. The angry growl that had arisen at his movement turned to laughter at his weakness. Too weary to care any more he lay in a state of semi-consciousness. He seemed to be at once floating through the dark and clinging mists of the marsh, and lying in the room hearing the low voices of the people whispering around him.

Gradually the sensation of floating became stronger and the consciousness of being in the room among strangers weaker. He could feel his limbs growing lighter and lighter. He was drifting upwards and he could feel the cold damp mist peeling downwards from his skin as he pushed up through it. He was aware of being above the swamp, rising higher still until he was, or seemed to be, in the sky looking down on the marshlands. From this height they were beautiful, the mists moving slowly, curling and spiralling, until patterns of great complexity were formed. Here and there beds of tall reeds rose through the mist, softened by it to fine, delicate black filaments. Above him the sky was deepening indigo, sparkling with the faint points of light which always appeared at twilight just before one star set and another rose.

The light was eerie and strangely dim, but it served for Bardek to see a great distance in every direction. The marshlands were widespread, but he was high enough to see beyond them to some low hills.

Even as he thought 'I must rise high to see beyond the hills', he felt himself rising. Amazed, he saw past the hills to the plains that he had been crossing when he had first been swept away. Further beyond them he could see the faint smudge of the mountains of his home.

He thought of Firilla.

Suddenly he was in a dark room, but not the one he knew himself to be still lying in, half-conscious. He was in his room at home and he knew that Firilla was lying on her bed. He could hear her breathing, but it was not the deep breathing of sleep.

As he stood quietly beside her he began to see everything in the room with perfect clarity as though it was light, though he could see no light source present. She was lying stiffly on her back, her eyes staring at the ceiling.

For a moment his heart lurched, thinking that she might be dead . . . but suddenly her eyes moved and she looked directly into his.

'Bardek!' she cried, rising towards him and reaching out her hands. 'Bardek!' He could feel her pain and her suffering in his own head as though it were his own. Then, with a sickening jerk, he found himself sitting up on the bed beside the youth, surrounded by strangers, his heart beating unnaturally fast.

He stared round, bewildered. The experience of being at home had been strong and vivid. It was as though his consciousness had split into separate sections, each one containing, somehow, the whole. Was it possible that we are 'everywhere' and 'everywhen' and just do not know it?

A woman offered him water ladled from a wooden pitcher and he drank thirstily, staring at the faces of those watching him. Had he been wrong about the violence and the hostility he had sensed there before? Had his first impressions of the marsh-dwellers been coloured by what he had been led to expect of them? Their faces were in some cases rough and unprepossessing, but their expressions at the moment were more curious and concerned than hostile.

He remembered the wounded youth and looked anxiously at him, but he looked now as though he was sleeping peacefully, and his arm and shoulder were bound with a combination of leaves and clean rags. On a brazier in the centre of the room a small fire burned, giving off greenish smoke, smelling strongly of herbs.

When he had finished drinking he was offered a coarse cereal in a bowl, and he ate it hungrily. Then he was given fish and bread. No words were spoken but he no longer felt he was among enemies.

When he could eat no more and had pushed the bowls away, shaking his head and smiling, the people seemed satisfied and most of them withdrew. Only the woman who had offered him the water and the fierce looking man with the red beard stayed close to him.

Bardek was wondering if they had a language in common and if he should be the first to speak, when the man himself spoke. He used the language Bardek was accustomed to, but with an unusual guttural intonation.

'Your tribe?' he asked. 'Your name?'

Bardek hesitated. He had no tribe. He was not even sure if he knew what a tribe was. The man's eyes narrowed. 'Bardek,' he answered hastily.

The man looked puzzled. 'I don't know of such a tribe.'

'It's not a tribe. It's my name.'

'Bardek?' The man repeated the name experimentally as though he had never heard anything like it before, and then he returned to the question that seemed of most importance to him. 'And what is your tribe?'

'I . . . I don't know.' The woman moved a step forward and stared very intently at him. 'I have no tribe,' Bardek said bleakly. Fear returned. He was wondering if he should invent a tribal name for himself when the youth beside him stirred at last and opened his eyes. The strangers turned their attention at once to him, and the others returned to watch him being given food and drink.

Feeling stronger, and wishing not to be so much at a disadvantage if trouble should arise, Bardek sat up slowly, testing his legs over the side of the bed, careful not to make any sudden movements to draw attention to himself. Gradually he lowered his feet to the floor and stood up, but dizziness made him sit down again, quickly.

He met the youth's eyes over the heads of the others and wondered if the boy would recognise him.

He did.

It was obvious these were not his people either. They were sizing him up in the same way they had done to Bardek, and the boy was looking at them with wary eyes.

'Your tribe? Your name?'

The same questions were growled.

'Py-yetti,' he answered in a low voice.

The man looked relieved. 'Your given name?'

'Negg.'

'That's good,' the leader said with satisfaction. 'We are friends of the people of the Py-yetti. We know of their village. But who is this companion of yours called Bardek? He says he has no tribe.'

Negg looked into Bardek's eyes. 'He lied,' he said calmly. 'He's of my tribe.'

'Why did you lie?' The man turned angrily to Bardek.

Bardek started to open his mouth though he had no idea what he was going to say, when Negg answered for him. 'He feared you were enemies of the Py-yetti.'

'He's a coward as well as a liar?'

'Not always,' Negg said. 'He fought two garrar beasts to save my life.'

The man was impressed and looked at Bardek with less hostility. 'Is this true?'

Bardek nodded dumbly. He thought it safer not to say anything but to leave the explanations to Negg who seemed to know what he was doing. He wondered if Negg had not just saved his life by claiming him as a member of his tribe. He must somehow contrive to be alone with him to talk, seeing him now as an ally and a friend. But Negg looked desperately pale and ill. The effort to think and speak had exhausted him, and he was lying back again with his eyes closed.

Bardek sat beside him feeling helpless. 'He must not die,' he thought. 'He must not die.' It seemed that Negg was his only hope of making some sense of the situation he found himself in; his only hope of escape from it.

'Negg,' he whispered, his lips almost to the youth's ear, his heart aching with all that they had been through together. 'Please live!'

The woman who had given water was the only one to hear. She touched his arm. 'He will live,' she said.

Although she, like her companions, was ragged and un-kempt, there was something different and special about her face. Bardek wondered if she had been born under a star other than the Dark Star. He had heard that sometimes chil-dren were born in the marshlands whose parents would not or could not take them to an Astrologer to be registered un-der their own birth Star and so they, like their parents, were doomed to live out their lives feared and forgotten and de-nied their rightful privileges.

The others who had been in the hut had now left to go about their business. Only the woman who had so intrigued him stayed with them. She fetched a twig from the brazier, one end of it burning and giving off a pungent spicy scent. She moved it carefully back and forth in front of Negg's nose so that he breathed in the smoke. Bardek watched with anxious interest, noticing that he himself was beginning to feel more rested and invigorated the more he breathed of the scented fumes.

Negg's cheeks gradually regained colour and his eyelids began to flicker.

'He's dreaming,' she said softly. 'Do you want to know what he is dreaming?'

'How can we know that until he wakes and tells us?'

She smiled. 'What do you want him to dream?'

Bardek looked puzzled.

'Think of something and he'll dream it.'

Bardek's thoughts involuntarily went back to when Negg had been fighting off the garrar beasts. The youth on the bed screamed and raised his arms to cover his face just as he done during the actual attack. Bardek was horrified. He had not meant to put Negg through that again; he had not believed for a moment that he could affect Negg's dreaming one way or another.

The woman gave him a sharp look as much as to say that he should watch his thoughts, and he determined not to think of the fight. But what could he think of? His mind seethed with all that had been happening. Negg's eyelids fluttered continuously and flickering expressions of pain and fear and bewilderment crossed his face from time to time, corresponding exactly to Bardek's thoughts.

'Stop it!' Bardek cried. 'I can't keep my thoughts under control and I don't want to affect his dreams.'

'Whether you want to or not, you do. It is the nature of thought that it passes from one to another. This it does more easily in sleep when all defences are down, particularly under the influence of this smoke.'

'Please, take it away!' Bardek cried as another jab of pain crossed Negg's face. 'I don't want to hurt him.'

'Choose well what you think, young man Bardek. It touches others and changes their lives.' Bardek tried to push the stick away. 'It is not just the smoke,' she said softly. 'The smoke facilitates. Have you ever noticed how a thought of yours has been picked up though no words have been spoken? '

He was silent. He had noticed it.

'Think healing thoughts . . . encouraging thoughts . . . positive thoughts. See him well and strong, striding the causeway, singing.'

Whether he was picking up her thoughts on the subject or whether he had mastered the skill himself he could not tell, but he found himself visualising Negg whole and healthy, walking beside him, journeying with him to the Temple of the White Star.

'Why do you go there,' the woman asked sharply, though he had not spoken. 'There is nothing but trouble there for the likes of us.' Bardek was shocked that she could see into his thoughts, but no longer surprised.

'I am not one of you,' he thought. 'I am a bowman, born under the Red Star.' The woman's eyes dilated. She seemed to be looking deep into his mind.

'You are one of us,' she said aloud. 'You were born at the time of the Dark Star.'

'No!'

She shrugged. 'Deny it if you will.'

'I would not deny it if it were true,' he said indignantly. 'It simply is not so.'

She turned away from him and returned the twig to the brazier. Bardek found himself sweating. He looked at Negg. Tears were seeping out from under his lids. Bardek bent over and shook him.

'Wake up! Negg, my friend, wake up. There is sorcery here and the sooner we get away from it the better.'

Negg woke up and looked with astonishment at Bardek's flushed and anxious face.

'If you take him now he might die,' the woman said.

'You said he would live.'

'If he rests and has the right treatment.'

'I want to get him back to his own people. There he will rest and get the right treatment.'

'As you wish,' she said casually. The room, apart from the three of them, was now empty.

'Can you stand?' Bardek asked Negg, who looked confused but remarkably much better. Bardek helped him up. 'Lean on me,' he said, and Negg leant on his shoulder. 'Can you walk?' Negg nodded.

'Eat first,' the woman said, holding out a platter of bread and cold fish. Negg looked hungrily at it, but he glanced first at Bardek as though asking permission.

'Eat,' said Bardek, nodding.

While Negg ate, the woman wrapped portions of bread

and fish and handed them to Bardek. 'Who knows how long your journey will be, Bardek of the Dark Star.' He flushed angrily, and she laughed. 'Take it, Bardek of the Mountains.'

There were many questions he would like to have asked, but Negg had finished eating and was pulling himself up again ready to go. He took the package of food and said nothing. The passage of thoughts between them seemed to be closed.

He helped Negg down the ladder and on to the causeway. The Indigo Star had risen fully now and the world was suffused in a dim purple light. 'Where are your people, Negg? Are they far from here?'

Negg did not at once reply but looked to the sky, the position of the Star. The mist had gone and they had a clear view of endless vistas of marshland. Bardek, used to mountains and landmarks, found it utterly disheartening. How could anyone ever find his way in this flat and desolate place? But Negg did not seem to share his discouragement; he looked as though he knew in which direction his home lay. 'We need the boat,' he said. 'Where is it?'

Bardek shrugged and shook his head. 'It could be anywhere,' he said helplessly. 'Somewhere along the main causeway. As soon as I found the path I abandoned the boat and walked. It was impossible to see,' he added defensively. 'There was a thick mist. I've no idea how long I was carrying you before I saw the light.'

Negg looked irritated. 'You must have noted something!'

Bardek could think of nothing. 'From what direction was the wind?'

'There was no wind.'

'You said the mist was moving.'

'It was curling round and round . . . it wasn't moving from one direction to another.'

Negg stumbled, and Bardek caught his uninjured arm. He suggested they rest, but Negg was stubbornly insistent that they press on. They passed the place where the small causeway joined the large and set off. But Negg's determination could not match his physical strength and they had to pause a while for him to rest. He demanded to know what Bardek had done with the bag that was in the punt. The young bowman told him he had left it where it was. Negg was furious. 'You expect me to believe that!' he said bitterly.

'I was carrying you. How could I have managed a bag as well?' Bardek was astonished at his companion's sudden bad temper and ingratitude. Negg looked at him with hard and suspicious eyes, drawing away. 'I left it in the boat! What else could I have done with it?'

'You could have hidden it to collect later.'

'I didn't touch it! Besides – what would I want with it?'

'Leaving it in the boat is bad enough,' grumbled Negg. 'Have you any idea how valuable those things are and how many people would give their lives to get their hands on them?'

'What things? I don't even know what was in the bag. The glimpse I had looked like precious metal, but . . .'

'Aha! So you did see what was in the bag!'

'Not really. A glimpse.'

'A glimpse is enough to make a greedy man greedier.'

'What were they and how did you come by them?'

'Never mind. But I'll kill you if we don't find them!'

'Kill me! When I've just saved your life? Kill me when you in fact have just saved mine?'

'I saved yours only because I thought you had the bag.'

'What's so special about those things?'

'They are the cult vessels of the Gaa-fen tribe, our greatest enemies. Without them they are powerless. With them we are powerful.'

'Cult vessels?'

'Are you so ignorant that you don't know the magic a tribe can put into its cult vessels? Are you so stupid that you think a people can be defeated by weapons alone?'

Bardek looked thoughtful. 'I am ignorant, my friend. I didn't know, though I suspected something of the kind. I wondered if you were a thief.'

'I am, and a good one too!' Negg said proudly, fiercely. 'I risked my life for those things and I'll not give them up.'

'Don't worry,' Bardek said. 'As soon as we find the boat you will have them. I didn't touch them. I swear it!'

Suddenly, a short distance away, a flock of whains rose from the reeds and flew screaming indignantly into the sky. Negg was instantly alert. 'There's someone there,' he whispered, ' . . .someone stealing our boat!'

Horrified, Bardek left his side and ran along the causeway. Negg was right: a man was trying to manoeuvre a boat through the reeds. Their boat! Without thinking, Bardek jumped from the wooden path into the water, forgetting that marsh water was not like the clear streams of his home. Not far below the greasy surface the liquid thickened to mud and a dense mass of slimy vegetation tangled round his legs. He floundered, every movement he made serving to sink him deeper into trouble. He cried out and the man turned to look at him. 'Now he'll get away!' thought Bardek desperately. His right arm was caught in the ribbons of a waterweed and in trying to free it he sank below the surface. The evil smelling water flooded into his mouth before he could shut it. Terrified, he thrashed about. He was almost losing consciousness when a hand fastened on his arm and held it tight, dragging him up. He thought he would be torn apart, the weed holding him so tight on one side, the hand on the other. But at last he got his head above water and could breathe again. Spluttering and spitting and gasping, he flailed about on the surface.

At first he did not realise quite what was happening, but when he did at last he found that it was the man in the boat, the man he had been about to attack, who was using his knife to hack at the weed that still held him and who was shouting at him to be still. Negg was above them on the causeway, also shouting for him to stop moving. His wild movements were endangering them both, churning up the water and rocking the boat. He held still at last, only his heart beating with fear, and his imagination conjuring up a dozen different images of death.

Once the water was calmer, the man succeeded quite easily in freeing him and hauling him into the boat. There they faced each other. Bardek saw now that he was quite an old man, lean and muscular, with white hair and face heavily lined. Negg was calling to him and he carefully turned the boat to pole it back to the causeway. He had made his own pole from a thick, tall reed, something Bardek might have thought to do when they fled from the fire had he not been so distraught.

Bardek sat hunched in the bottom of the boat, shivering with the shock of what he had just been through, relieved to see that the bag was still in the bottom of the boat where he had last seen it, ashamed that his actions had been so violent and thoughtless. He remembered how he had rushed unthinkingly to try to rescue the girl in the Temple. When would he learn to think with his head and not his feet? Everything depended on thought. Without it, man is less than he need be.

When they drew near, Negg and the stranger greeted each other like old friends. Bardek could not quite understand all that was being said as they were speaking in a dialect that only partially resembled his own, but he could see from their expressions and the gestures of the old man that the news he brought was not good. Negg became very agitated and pointed at the bag. The old man lifted it and handed it to him. Negg stood for a moment with it held high above his head, his face transfigured with hate, shrieking out what Bardek could only think was a fearsome curse, and then, with all his strength he flung the package he had risked his life to steal as far as he could. Astonished, Bardek saw it lie on the surface of the thick water for a moment, the metal gleaming richly, and then sink with a horrible sound as though it had been sucked down by some awful dark deep-water creature.

'What is it? What has happened?' he asked, bewildered.

Negg slumped to the wooden planks, exhausted, his face drawn and pale, a kind of hopelessness now in his expression that Bardek had not seen before. 'What is the news you bring?' he demanded of the old man.

He shook his head, his face very grim. 'We no longer have a tribe. We are wanderers with all the world against us. We'll soon be dead.'

'What do you mean?'

'Our enemies, the Gaa-fen, attacked and destroyed all our people, all our homes,' Negg interrupted bitterly. 'He was the only one to escape. He and I have no home, no tribe to go back to. If only I had been in time with the cult vessels!'

Bardek had seen enough of the ways of the marsh-people to know how important belonging to a tribe was to them. He also realised, from his own point of view, how difficult this could make his escape from the marshes. He had expected help from Negg's tribe. He refrained from saying that in his opinion it was probably the stealing of the precious cult vessels that had set the Gaa-fen on the warpath in the first place. What did he know of the intricacies of inter-tribal enmity? He knew only that such enmity rarely had reason on its side.

'Could we not go back to the people we just left?' he asked. 'They claimed to be friends of the Py-yetti. They might take you in.'

Both the old man and the young shook their heads. 'They were only our friends when the Py-yetti were powerful and they needed us as allies,' Negg said. 'Now that we are of no use to them, they would kill us as soon as look at us.'

'You did not kill me. You rescued me,' Bardek said to the old man, 'though I am not of your tribe and am of no use to you.'

'I rescued you only because my tribesman Negg told me to.'

'And why did you tell him to?' Bardek asked Negg.

'Because I was not sure if the bag was still in the boat . . .'

'If what was in the bag was so precious why did you throw it away?'

'Because my curse is now on those garrar-piss Gaa-fen and they will never be able to lift it!'

Bardek was silent, uncomfortable in the face of such hate.

Time passed. The three men sat on the causeway for a long time before anyone said anything more. At last they started to consider what courses were open to them.

'You must leave me, I am dying,' said Negg at last. 'The two of you take the boat and live as eels, moving about as long as you can avoid enemies.'

'That is the only way,' the old man said with resignation.

'We cannot leave you,' cried Bardek. 'What are you thinking of,' he shouted at the old man. 'If we are wanderers and outcasts we will be wanderers and outcasts together – the three of us.'

'He'll slow us up! His weight in the boat . . . and he'll not be capable of helping us in any way . . .'

Bardek was furious. 'I will not abandon him. He must come with us.'

'Don't be foolish my friend, think of yourself,' Negg said.

'I am thinking of myself. We have been brought together in ways I do not understand, for reasons I do not understand. Who knows how my fate is tied up with yours! Besides . . .' he added, 'I know you and I don't know this man.'

'My name is Millon,' the old man said, as though by knowing his name he would know him.

'Mine is Bardek – but that tells you nothing about myself.'

'You are a bowman, though it looks as though your tribe has thrown you out. And we are marsh-dwellers, members of a dead tribe. Knowing that, we know everything we need to know about each other.'

Bardek frowned. He might have accepted this a little while ago. But not now. There was another silence between them for a while until Bardek broke it. 'Do you mean to tell me that just because your tribe is destroyed you are going to wander round and round in these marshes until you drop dead or something eats you, with no other purpose in life than to avoid being killed or captured?'

'What else is there for us?'

Bardek threw up his hands. 'I could speak all day and never exhaust what else there is!'

'Name one thing,' said Negg faintly, he had slumped onto the rough black wood of the causeway and looked very near to death, more from despair than from his wounds.

'You could come with me. I for one do not intend to spend the rest of my life as you suggest. I am going to get out of these marshes and find my way to Bar-geda. Once there I am going to the Temple of the White Star and I am going to find a girl I saw there and ask her some questions.'

Negg raised his head and his eyes flashed with interest. 'Even if we find our way out of the marshes, which is impossible, how would we live away from them? We know no other life.'

'Then it's time you learned one,' Bardek said firmly.

'But we were born under the Dark Star and we cannot go to Bar-geda. It is forbidden.'

'Who forbids it?'

'The priests of the very Temple you say you are going to visit.'

Negg had touched on another question that had begun to trouble Bardek. 'I have seen the priests you are so much in awe of,' he said. 'And I am not sure they deserve to be obeyed.' There was a gasp from the old man, but Negg was fascinated and sat up to listen. 'They are holding a young girl prisoner. I saw her and she called on me for help. I have decided that if it kills me I am still going to try to save her.'

Negg was very excited. 'Why do we not go too, Millon?' he cried. 'We may die anyway. Is it not more interesting to try to do something before we die?'

Millon was still hesitating.

'What have you to lose?' Bardek said bluntly.

What indeed?

'And as for your worry about what you do outside the marshes, leave that to me. Your task will be to guide us through. For here I am at a disadvantage. But once outside . . .'

Negg grinned. 'Then we'll see what mountain dwellers are made of, eh?'

Millon shrugged and agreed to go. Not because he believed that Bardek's quest had any chance of success, but because, as Negg said, it would be more interesting, if no less dangerous, than the alternative.

The way out of the marshes was not easy to find but, with Millon's years of experience to help, they reached a place at last where even Bardek could see a movement in the water, indicating that a current was flowing, however sluggishly, towards the south.

They followed this course for a long time, eating eels and wild whains to sustain themselves, and chewing on the stems of certain plants that the marsh dwellers knew were nourishing and thirst quenching. Bardek insisted on resting whenever Negg needed to rest, and this in itself delayed them. But whether it was because Negg now had a purpose, or whether it was because Bardek, remembering what he had learned about thought, kept thinking of him as whole and well, Negg's youth and resilience began to pay off and he had recovered completely by the time the reed beds and sedges began to give way to grasslands and hills.

From then on, to Bardek's relief, they relied on their own legs for the journey and the food they had was either trapped by him or gathered under his supervision from plants he knew more about. Once or twice they came upon an isolated village and the marsh dwellers hid while Bardek asked directions, returning to them at last laden with provisions generously given.

CHAPTER 6

The Cage of Crystal

Before they reached Bar-geda, Bardek told Negg and Millon all he knew about the town. On the outskirts he left them hidden while he slipped in to find some suitable clothes for them. Those they were wearing, rough breeches sewn from the pelts of water rats and ragged jackets that had known better days on the backs of city dwellers, would have given them away as marsh dwellers to be shunned and feared. Bardek exchanged a gold chain Firilla had given him, and which he always wore on his wrist, for some clothes in hunter's red, and some good food.

On his return he tried to make the two seem less wild and conspicuous. They buried their rags, but kept their belt knives, their pouches of fire powder and the other oddments they thought they might need. When he was satisfied that they looked like bowmen, Bardek led them confidently through the streets as though he were a natural city dweller.

Surprisingly quickly they found the road that led to the base of the outcrop on which the Temple of the White Star stood. He pointed and they looked up. The white rock of the hill with its clinging trenoids and cliffs rose before them so high they had to lean back to see the summit. From this angle they couldn't see the whole Temple, but its tallest crystal towers gleamed and shone, almost in the sky.

The marsh dwellers were speechless.

'There is a way up,' Bardek said, 'although from here it doesn't look as though there is.'

'You're not getting me up there,' muttered Millon.

'Nor me!' said Negg.

Bardek looked at them in surprise. 'But this is what we've come for. The girl I told you about, the prisoner, is up there.'

'She's your girl, you rescue her!' said Negg, turning to walk away.

Bardek caught his arm. 'Where are you going?'

'Now that we're bowmen,' Negg said with a grin, 'I should think we'd go and find us girls of our own.'

'But . . .'

'I've always wanted to see the city,' Millon said.

Negg shook himself free of Bardek's hand and began to move away again, Millon with him. 'Stop!' Bardek cried. 'You promised to help me.'

They stopped and looked at him. 'Promised?' they said, a touch of mocking disbelief in their voices.

'Well, you said . . .'

'Ah, *said!*' laughed Negg.

'The hill is too steep,' Millon said. 'And even if we did get up it, the Temple at the top would be too much for us to tackle.'

'Why don't you forget the girl and come with us?' Negg said.

Bardek was silent, angry. No wonder marsh dwellers were despised! 'I would think you owed me something for saving your life,' he said at last, bitterly, ashamed of himself for saying it as soon as the words were out.

The two marsh dwellers looked at him. They had stopped smiling. 'Do you take our lives upon you, Bardek of the Mountains?' Millon asked coldly.

'What does that mean?'

'You take responsibility for everything we are or do.' Negg said. 'As though we are within your own cage of bone.'

'And if I do,' Bardek asked wildly, 'will you help me?'

'We would have no choice.'

'Then I do!' he cried.

Millon pursed his lips and squinted up the steep hill to the shimmering crystal at the summit. 'My death is your death,' he murmured. 'Your death is my death.'

'Wait a moment,' said Bardek hastily. He looked from one to the other. 'What is this custom? What am I committing myself to for your help?'

'We are your limbs. Use us,' Millon said enigmatically.

Bardek looked at them uneasily. They had been through much together and he had assumed they were his friends. But now there was something about them he could not understand. He realised that however well he thought he knew them, he didn't know them at all. He didn't want extra limbs, he wanted companions . . .

He cleared his throat. 'I don't want to take your lives upon me! They are yours. I want your help, freely, as friends.'

Negg and Millon looked at each other.

'Then freely, as friends,' Negg said, suddenly cheerful again, 'we refuse to help you.' And this time he turned and walked briskly down the road, with Millon following him, before Bardek could remonstrate further.

Frustrated and angry he watched them until they were out of sight and then he turned back to the hill.

Well, he was on his own again, as he had been when he set out. He had had no thought of anyone's help when he decided to seek the girl and he would manage without anyone's help now. This time he would not loose his head and go rushing around the Temple like a startled fear-all. He would use his mind.

When he reached the rock platform on which the Temple stood, he hesitated for a while at the edge, half hidden by the bushes and trenoids, half by the fountains, observing and thinking. And then he moved forward cautiously, still uneasy as to whether the figures walking along the transparent corridors and through the translucent halls could see him or not.

He found that the skull was still in the first hall, but it was alone, without ceremonial. He looked along the tall shining walls and still saw no sign of a door or a break in either direction. Slowly, carefully, quietly, he made his way around the Temple, searching every crystal surface meticulously. Nothing.

He suddenly thought of the Marsh Seer. What she had been doing among the marsh people he did not know, for Seers and Psychics were usually under the patronage of the White Star. But what she had said about the power of thought, and his own experiences when he had 'visited' Firilla, came back to him now and helped him to form a plan.

If he was capable of those few amazing feats without any training, how much more would the priests of the White Star be capable of. It was possible that they did not have a door to their temple, because they did not need one. They could probably pass freely wherever they wanted to go, just by thinking about it.

The flesh at the roots of his hair prickled as he realised the kind of adversaries they would be with such a capacity. But then he thought boldly: if they could do it, so could he! He did not know from where he received this sudden wave of self-confidence, but he was grateful for it. He noticed a blasphemous, rebellious thought stirring in the back of his mind. Why should he be tied to the Red Star of his birth? He had yearnings to be much more than a hunter. He had never in fact enjoyed hunting, but had forced himself to do it because it was expected of him. He felt his mind stretching and reaching beyond himself, desiring the knowledge of the White Priesthood, longing for their capacities, their powers.

He shut his eyes.

Carefully, painstakingly, he recreated in his mind every detail of the immense crystal edifice before him. He did not know where the girl was, so he concentrated on the external walls, and settled at last to one particular face, working at it with his mind, imagining a needle point of white fire tracing an arced line over and over again on the same area.

Gradually his concentration grew steadier. No distractions drew his attention away. The beam of thought he was using cut through the crystal, and he saw himself, as though in a dream, leaping through the hole he had made into the deserted hall beyond. He found his heart was pounding and his head was aching with the effort he had just made.

He opened his eyes, believing himself to be within the building. He was. He could not see the hole through which he had come, for it had ceased to be as soon as he stopped thinking about it. The wall was whole again, but he was on the other side of it, standing on smooth white marble, white light shimmering round him.

He could not see through the wall to the outside world. It was as though nothing existed outside the Temple. He lifted his eyes and looked with awe up and up the shining walls to where the ceiling must surely be. But where he expected solidity he found only light; light so dazzling he could not see through it. He shivered with pleasure remembering a time in the mountains when he had plunged into a very deep pool and seen this same dazzling, shimmering intensity of light as he rose to the surface.

He could have stood gazing around him forever, forgetting his mission, had not the very beauty of the place reminded him of the girl he had come to find.

He stepped forward and found that he could move easily over the smooth paving stones, almost gliding without sound or effort. He was glad of this for he did not want to be found by the priests in their holy of holies. He left the hall, moving as swiftly as he could along the corridors, avoiding any that seemed too exposed or had the shadow of people in them. Having no notion of the inner construction of the Temple, he could not visualise it as he had the outside, but he noticed that some of the crystal of the inner walls had imperfections in it which made it less transparent. He kept to these corridors and rooms as much as he could, dodging and sliding, penetrating deeper and deeper into the heart of the building.

As he travelled further and further away from the outer halls, the light changed. It was still white, but it glimmered rather than shone. He could not see as clearly or as far. It was getting colder too, as though he were going deeper and deeper into a block of ice, the light occasionally taking on a greenish or a bluish tint. He shivered again, but with cold this time.

It was strange. He felt as though he were at the heart of darkness and yet everywhere the light was still glimmering. There were no doors, no furniture, he came upon no people. It was a desolate, eerie place – beautiful beyond words, but without life.

He was beginning to wonder if in fact he was not in the building at all, but still hiding on the rim of the hill, and all this was taking place in his mind, when he heard a sound and decided to follow it. In a place that surely must have been at the centre of the labyrinth of corridors and rooms was a vast hall, entirely empty but for a tall crystal standing in the centre. He found himself drawn to it by a sudden sense of urgency.

He gasped.

Inside the crystal, as though preserved in ice, was a body – that of the girl he was seeking!

He ran forward, the gliding movement that had come so easily giving way to clumsiness. He almost tripped in his eagerness, though the floor had no obstacles to trip him. He went round and round the crystal, his mind in turmoil, the coldness of the place beginning to reach into his heart, tapping it, pulling at it, trying to break it open. But it was impregnable.

Her silver hair was flowing out behind her as though she had been caught in mid-movement. One hand was raised in a gesture of appeal. Her eyes were open and, although they did not move, he was convinced she could see him.

He wanted to call to her, but he did not know her name. Helplessly he stood and stared at her, the palms of his hands on the cold crystal, his face close to hers.

Suddenly he remembered how he had broken into the building in the first place. He was a bowman, but he had already tapped a secret knowledge only the seers and psychics had. Could he use it again?

He tried to calm himself and stand back from the girl. He

shut his eyes and concentrated his attention on breaking open the crystal that held her so cruelly prisoner. It was only when he felt that his own mind would break in two if he persisted a moment longer that he opened his eyes expecting to see her free. But she was not. Nothing had changed. Matter had not submitted itself this time to rearrangement under the mysterious and potent energy of thought. And yet . . . something had changed. Now, within his head, he heard the girl's thoughts as clearly as if she were speaking them aloud.

'Help me! Help me! Please . . . please . . . help me!'

He felt a pain and a despair greater than he had ever felt before, and a loneliness beyond all loneliness.

'I'll get you out of there!' he cried. 'Help me. Tell me what I must do!'

Her voice seemed to shriek in his head and he clapped his hands over his ears as though that would keep it out, crouching on the ground, rocking backwards and forwards, moaning, the pain almost unendurable. It felt as though his mind was being taken over by several different minds. Thoughts that were not his own were crowding in on him. It was as though he were hearing the voice of the girl across a crowded room, a room in which everyone present was shouting at everyone else . . .

'Stop it!' he cried. 'Stop it!' But 'they' did not stop and 'he' did not know how to make them. He could no longer tell which were his feelings and which were hers, which were his thoughts or which were the thoughts of those 'others'. He knew only that he would go insane if the cacophony kept up much longer.

Suddenly there was silence.

Bardek sank to the floor with exhaustion and relief. He was free. He was himself again. He looked up at her and saw that she was still encased and that from a door on the other side of the hall to him figures were beginning to emerge. He knew that if he were caught he would never be able to help her. He half rose and with a swiftness that surprised him he slid across the floor towards the opposite door and out into the corridor. No one challenged him. Perhaps the priests were so little on their guard because to them it was unthinkable that any stranger could penetrate the Temple. On Agaron, everyone knew his or her place and kept to it, and no one but those born to it would dream of approaching, let alone entering, the Temple of the White Crystal. The dim shadow of Bardek could have been seen through the walls if they had chosen to look. But they did not. Secure in their hierarchy they circled the crystal, chanting one word softly and ceaselessly. Bardek leaned forward trying to understand the word. 'Vallida . . . Vallida . . . Vallida.' What did it mean? Sometimes it was as soft as a whisper, at other times it rose to a shout, but it always flowed in waves of sound to wash against the crystal cage, building up a vibrationary force which eventually he felt sure must break the crystal open.

Suddenly the moment came and Bardek saw the walls of the crystal dissolve into light and the girl released. Her silver hair fell to her back as though only a second before it had been disturbed. She turned, the white silk of her dress floating free around her like a filmy cloud of shining mezmer seeds. A tall priest stepped forward and took her hand. 'Vallida,' he said one more time and Bardek realised it was her name. 'Vallida?' he thought, and then aloud he said it again. She looked beyond the priests and met his eyes. Her face was full of joy. Before they realised what was happening she had slipped away from them and run across the room to Bardek. He took her arm and together they fled, the priests at first too astonished to move.

'This way!' she cried, her voice reminding him of mountain water after rain. He followed her down corridors that all seemed the same, hoping she knew where she was going. They both knew that they only had this one chance. Bardek could imagine what the penalty would be for the sacrilege of breaking into the sacred Temple of the White Star and kidnapping its Oracle, for Oracle he now realised she must be.

They burst out at last into the lightest hall of all, that of the crystal skull. Bardek made at once for the outer wall, hoping he had enough strength of mind left to control the beam of thought necessary to break out as he had broken in. 'Not there!' he heard her shout. 'Help me here! Help me!'

He looked round in time to see her trying to push the crystal skull from its plinth.

'What are you doing? There's no time for that!'

'If I don't destroy it, I'll never be free!'

Bardek hesitated, shocked. Freeing a beautiful prisoner in distress was one thing, destroying the most central holy image of the greatest Temple on the planet was another. 'Leave it,' he cried. 'Let us get away!'

'No. No! Help me!' Her voice was frantic and he could see that she would never dislodge the giant skull by herself. He rushed back to her side and was just about to lift his hands to help when she suddenly turned on him. She was transformed. A fierce and terrifying being seemed to be looking out of her eyes and her voice roared out loud and masculine, echoing through the hall like thunder.

'Touch the Holy Sepulchre of the gods at your peril, Bardek, son of the Dark Star!'

He was horrified by the change in her and by the fact that she had associated him with the Dark Star. Black ice seemed to be taking the place of blood in his veins.

Child of the Dark Star?

So be it.

He pulled back from her and turned to the Skull. If Vallida said that she would only be free if it were destroyed, he would destroy it. Children of the Dark Star were children of Destruction. He would dare anything.

He raised his hands.

She struck him across the face, her hands like stone.

'I will tear your liver out and feed it to my garrar beasts. You will live on but you will plead for death . . .'

Her voice was different now, high and shrill, neither her own nor that of he who had spoken before.

'Vallida!' he screamed as he tried to fight her off. And as

suddenly as the strange voice had started, so suddenly it ceased.

Bewildered, she stared at him as he seized her arm and pulled her to the outer wall. Just as the priests broke into the hall he directed his will with immense passion to the crystal and was through it, still holding her arm, before the men had crossed the floor. Even then their pursuers might still have seized them had not a hail of stones greeted them as soon as they emerged. With joyful astonishment Bardek saw that the stone-throwers were none other than Negg and Millon.

'Run!' shouted Negg. 'Take her to safety!'

Bardek did not stop to question, but ran with her through the fountains to the outer rim of the platform, pushing her unceremoniously down the slope beyond it.

They scrambled and slid, dislodging pebbles, breaking twigs, soon to be followed by the triumphant marsh dwellers, the priests having retreated under the barrage of stones.

At the bottom of the hill they looked at each other. Negg, Millon and Bardek were scratched and dusty and sweating, their eyes shining with excitement, but behind the excitement the shadow of uncertainty as to what to do next was growing.

They looked at the girl.

She seemed to be untouched by the rough passage down the hill. The glowing silk of her dress was unmarked, her silver hair unruffled. No dust or sweat marred her fine pale skin; only the expression on her face showed that she was no longer contained in the crystal world at the top of the hill. She turned her head slowly, her eyes drinking in all there was to see. Across her face played the emotions of wonder, awe, fear and astonishment. Bardek realised that it was probable she had never been outside the Temple, and suddenly he had a twinge of doubt that he had done the right thing in seizing her and forcing her out into the world.

The huge dome of the sky directly above them was a deep, rich purple, shot through with beams of pale violet light that radiated from the centre of the Star. The air around them was dim; soft and thick as velvet. Shadows were holding each distant feature of the landscape separate, cupped in purple darkness.

No one moved in the town. It was the time for sleep. They heard the far, far cry of a merrow-whain, the most beautiful sound of the sky.

'Come,' Bardek said urgently. 'We can't stay here.'

He took Vallida's hand and gently pulled her after him. He wanted to get as far away as possible from the Temple. They passed through the outskirts of the town unseen, the streets deserted, the lids of all eyes but their own shut against the light. From time to time they looked uneasily over their shoulders, but no one pursued them. Negg and Millon were delighted about this and put it down to the effectiveness of their rock throwing, but Bardek was uneasy. Why were they not pursued? Vallida was their Oracle – without her their power in the community would be diminished. Firilla had once told him that the Oracle dictated what was to be done in every serious crisis. It was more powerful than the Governors, its Voice overrode all Laws.

It was her horoscope that had imprisoned Vallida in her role as Oracle. Her conception had been arranged. Her mother, the High Priestess of the Temple of the Blue Star, herself born at the most propitious moment during the time of the Blue Star's greatest influence, had been subjected to ritual impregnation by the six most important men in the hierarchy of the White Star's priesthood, so that no man could claim paternity. The moment for this ritual had been chosen very carefully by the astrologers. The moment of her birth watched for anxiously. If she was born as predicted at the time of the White Star's greatest influence, her mother would return to the Blue Temple and resume her role as High Priestess. If the time of her birth had varied in any way from the predicted horoscope, she and her mother would never have been heard of again.

Bardek looked at the girl walking beside him, her hand trustingly in his, the softness of her bare arm brushing against his arm, her hair swinging against his shoulders. She saw him looking at her and smiled at him, a little shyly, as though she too were looking at him for the first time, and liked what she saw.

Negg suddenly startled them by smashing a shop window and seizing a cloak that was displayed there. Bardek looked horrified; it did not strike him that smashing through the walls of the highest temple in the land and stealing its most precious treasure was similar to Negg's action. He had been told that stealing was evil, and belonged only to the Children of the Dark Star. He looked angrily at Negg, who laughed cheerfully and shrugged. 'She needs a cloak. How else can we get one?'

This was true. As she was she could not move anywhere without causing a sensation. Apart from her natural beauty, which was considerable, she had a strange soft glow about her which made her radiate light. Her shining silver hair, flowing almost to her knees, was like no other woman's. It alone would have drawn people's eyes to them.

Negg lifted the cloak as though to put it on Vallida and then hesitated. He looked at Bardek. 'Here,' he said gruffly, handing him the cloak, and turned quickly away as though being so close to her had disturbed him more than he liked.

Bardek took the cloak. Its fabric was well woven and smooth, but even so it seemed too rough to put round this creature of air and light. He knew however that Negg was right, and lifted the cloak and lowered it onto her shoulders. As he did so his hands touched her, and he was overwhelmed by such a strong desire to hold her even closer that if Millon had not called out that he had heard someone coming he would not have been able to keep control of himself. The girl's eyes had been clear and wondering. There had been no response in them to the passion that was revealed in his. Perhaps she had no understanding of what such a passion could mean.

The cloak covered her safely from head to toe. Bardek took her hand again and they started to run. After being able to move so swiftly and so easily in the Temple, the hard ground and the obstacles they now so constantly encountered seemed very irritating and frustrating. Negg and Millon on the other hand, who had known only the marshlands before this, found the sensation of running over firm ground exhilarating.

In the Temple of the Blue Star on the hill opposite the Temple of the White Star, at the other side of the city, the priestesses were preparing for the Ceremony of Waking. The High Priestess Maya, Vallida's mother, was mounting the steps of lapis lazuli and blue marble to take her place on the high sapphire throne.

Still as beautiful as the day she was sent to the Temple of the White Star to conceive an Oracle, her body showed through the flowing blue ribbons of her gown as she climbed from step to step. Once at the top, immensely high above the others, on a throne in the domed roof of blue crystal, she arranged the ribbons around her to fall gracefully and modestly to the floor. She fitted her head into the crown of spiked mirror-stone that stayed always in position above the throne, and sighed as the clasping weight of it pressed upon her brow.

From her position in the dome she could see out into the world. The city of Bar-geda lay below her in all its sprawling untidiness. She could see the city's other six hills. The five holding temples, the sixth with its dark obsidian obelisk marking the place where the Temple of the Dark Lord had once stood before a former generation had been told by the Oracle to destroy it.

The plains that stretched beyond the town made her long for freedom. Beyond them, at the furthest reach of her sight to the west, lay mountains. She sometimes dreamed of those rocky peaks, seeing herself flying over them, her wings outstretched like the greatest of the whains, drifting on air currents, her eyes straining to see and her memory to hold every glimpse of the rich variety of rock and plant that made up this varied and intriguing landscape. She sometimes dreamed of being with her daughter, the two of them living as ordinary people lived. But she was not free. She had duties, responsibilities.

She turned her attention to the Temple of the White Star and what she saw there caused her to draw in her breath sharply. Instead of shining serenely and steadily as it always did and had done since the beginning of memory, it was alternately giving off a harsh glare and a faltering flicker of light and dark.

She stared as hard as she dared without alarming the priestesses in the hall below. Usually its light was too bright for a direct gaze. But now only in flashes did it have its old magnificence. Something was wrong.

Before she could stop herself, her thoughts rushed to her daughter, the girl she had never seen, for even at the moment of birth, lest she see her and love her, she had been blindfolded, and lest she should reach for her and love her by touching her, her hands had been clamped above her head. She knew now intuitively that her daughter was somehow involved in what was happening, and her heart began to race with the kind of agitation a High Priestess should not feel. All this time as High Priestess and she was still prey to the emotions of a common woman!

Angrily she tried to bring her heart under control, knowing that there was very little time before her priestesses would be taking up their positions for the ceremony. 'My child! My child!' her heart cried, while her mind strained to hold to the ritual words that were expected of her.

If the unthinkable had happened, and the acolytes of the White Star were in trouble, it was even more important that she and her Order hold firm to the ancient pattern.

On each arm of the throne were her symbols of office, to be used at the appropriate time in the ceremony. 'Children of the Stars of Light, the time of resting is done,' she cried after the invocation for the protection of the gods, and lifting the orb of mirror-stone from the right of the throne, she fitted it into the rod of silver from the left, and held it above her head. The priestesses below her in the hall began to sing, and as their song reached a kind of ecstasy she started to spin the orb, until at the height of the song it caught the light from the Star and magnificently, dazzlingly, it magnified it and beamed it out across the city, a flashing beacon of purple and white that penetrated the blinds and curtains of the sleeping populace and told them it was time to awake and to go about their business. Few questioned why the sleeping time and the waking time were as they were. Only the High Priests knew that the rules for them had been laid down by their remote ancestors, the Earthmen who had landed on this desolate world in the ancient days. Finding that their biological need to rest and sleep no longer fitted neatly into a pattern of night following day and day following night as it had on their own small planet, they chose to follow a pattern of sleep and waking that felt comfortable to them irrespective of whether there was light or dark. The period of each star was different; some were in the sky for only one period of sleep and waking; others, the Indigo and the Blue, exceeded that, while the period of the White was longest of all. It was to the needs of their own physical bodies that those ancient people set the rhythms of sleep and waking — not to the pattern of the rising and setting of the heavenly bodies.

The little group of fugitives just entering the desert plains to the west of the city were almost blinded as the light flashed through them, the girl alone not finding it necessary to stop and rub eyes, and blink, and wonder if there was permanent damage or not.

'Hurry,' she said to Bardek, taking his arm and tugging at him. He had let her hand go as the light swung over them, and was now standing with his head bent upon his hands, moaning slightly.

He pulled himself together. He knew that they should be

well out of sight of the city by the time the people awoke. The time of the Star of Indigo was not a bad time to be on the run. It's predominant influence was towards creativeness, and although, in order to be creative, a certain amount of drive and aggression was necessary, the people on the whole were content to turn their hands to art forms or music, to carpentry and weaving, and were unlikely to pursue strangers with hostility. But Bardek knew that he had tampered with a fundamental part of the very Law that kept the pattern predictable and safe. It was possible that they would no longer be able to rely on things as they had before, nor on the friendliness of that particular time. They began to run.

Negg and Millon had stolen some food, and when they felt they were far enough from the city they sat and ate. 'I can't understand why the priests are not pursuing us,' Bardek gave voice at last to something that had been troubling him all the time.

'Perhaps they don't know what to do,' Vallida said gently. 'They have grown so used to listening to my Voices and obeying their commands, without them they are lost.'

'What are these "voices"?' Bardek asked, recalling his terrible experience in the chamber of the crystal skull.

Vallida shuddered, her eyes so full of distress that he did not have the heart to question her further.

'Never mind,' he said hastily. 'There will be time enough later.'

'If there is a "later",' Negg said gloomily.

Bardek gave him a sharp look. 'Of course there will be a later!'

'Where is there to go?' Negg demanded. 'The Temple power reaches everywhere.'

'The marshes. No one dares the marshes,' said Millon, a touch of pride in his voice, for he was at home there. 'They have been abandoned to the Children of the Dark Star.'

'You forget we have no tribe to protect us.' Negg said. 'But perhaps we could start our own tribe,' he added, with a quizzical look at Vallida.

Catching his meaning, Bardek stood up at once. 'We're going to the mountains,' he said firmly.

'The mountains?'

'Yes. My home. My mother will take care of Vallida until . . .'

'Your mother . . .' said the girl with a great longing in her voice.

'Yes, we'll be safe there. Until I came to Bar-geda I never felt the power of the priests. Nature rules in the mountains. You learn its ways and it is easy to survive.'

'But mountains . . .' said Millon doubtfully. The city had seemed strange, but mountains would be even stranger.

'Come on, you old eel-brain,' said Negg cheerfully. 'It will be good to try a new way of living for a change. If Bardek can survive there, anybody can,' and he gave a laugh. Bardek punched him playfully.

'I never did thank you for coming to my rescue,' Bardek said as they started walking again. 'I don't think we would have escaped if you'd not been waiting there with those stones.'

Negg started to whistle, stepping out ahead of them briskly.

'Come to think of it,' Bardek said to Millon. 'Why did you come back for me? You endangered your own lives. Surely that is against your basic instincts?'

Millon shrugged. 'I would not have come, but Negg thought it would be fun.'

'Fun!'

'He was not wrong,' said Millon drily.

Vallida, walking slightly ahead of Bardek as though she were eager to reach the mountains, loosened the cloak and let it drop from her shoulders. The white silk she wore looked almost violet in the light of the purple Star, but her hair still shone fine and silver.

Bardek stopped and picked up her cloak and speeded up to keep pace with her. It might be too warm for the cloak now, but she would need it later. They walked in silence for a long time, thinking their own thoughts.

They had travelled a good distance across the plain when a shadow suddenly passed over them.

The sudden chill made them look up. Above them, wheeling slowly, were three garrar beasts.

Bardek looked around. There was no cover. They were too far from the town to even think of running back to it and too far from the mountains to reach the shelter of rocks or caves. He had no bow, but his knife was still at his belt.

They stood still, looking upwards, three of them at least knew what those dark shapes foretold.

'If we stay absolutely still,' Bardek suggested, 'we may not be noticed. It is the movement of prey that alerts the hunter.'

'We've already been seen,' Negg said. 'See the centre of their spiral is on us.'

The beasts were lowering with each turn of the circle.

'There is still nothing to do but stand and wait for them,' Millon said. 'There's nowhere to hide. We have knives. There are three of us and three of them. Pray to your Star, bowman. There is nothing else will save us now.'

Lower and lower came the dread figures, their wings cutting out the light. Bardek held the girl's cloak in one hand, his knife in the other. 'Keep close together,' he said. 'We mustn't be separated. If one of us is alone he will certainly be seized.' He turned to Vallida. 'Do you understand?' he said. 'Whatever you do keep close to us. Duck and dodge. Try to keep out of the way of both the knives and the claws.'

She was staring up at the beasts with a wondering, thoughtful expression. 'They are very dangerous,' Bardek said to her, worried and impatient that she did not seem to be afraid. 'If we are killed they will kill you.'

She stood quite still, looking upwards. 'If we are killed and you are left alone, run backwards and forwards, round and round. Keep moving, but never in a straight line. They're very cumbersome creatures and can't turn quickly. If we can wound them, they might tire and leave you alone.' He was talking as though he thought there was no possibility that the three of them would survive the attack.

Suddenly a beast swooped.

They could feel the rush of hot air as its wings passed them, but strangely its claws and beak did not reach for them. It was so close that they could see the veins in its red eye, but it did no more than beat its wings so that the wind it created knocked them off balance.

Then another plunged.

Shouting as loud as they could the three men struggled to keep upright, and flailed about with their knives, trying to get purchase on the fearsome dark bodies. They were buffeted from side to side, choked by the dust of the dry plain that rose with the close beating of the giant wings. Confused and terrified they fought on, but never drew blood, never touched the beasts hide nor tore a feather from their wings.

Suddenly it was all over. The three men were on the ground, coughing and spluttering, unharmed. The dark wings of the beasts no longer came between them and the light of the Star. Bewildered, Bardek lifted his head. He felt no pain and had no wounds.

A little way from where he lay, back in the direction of Bar-geda, he saw Vallida walking calmly, the three great dark beasts flying and swooping over her head but never touching her. It seemed to Bardek that they were driving her towards the town as though they were shepherding her. The wind caused by their wings was lifting the soft silk of her dress so that it billowed out around her, and her hair was separated into a million strands of silver, riding around her head like the aura of a Star.

'No!' he cried, the pain in his heart at the thought of losing her too great to bear.

Without thinking, he staggered to his feet and started to run after her. He had dropped his knife, but he thought of nothing but being with her.

'Vallida!' he called. 'Vallida!'

At the sounding of her name she turned and reached her

arms towards him. But even as she did so a terrible spasm of pain passed through her body and distorted her face. She raised her arms above her head. Her face became that of a stranger, and her voice when she spoke was fierce and huge.

'Go back, Child of the Dark Star. Your death is not yet required of you!'

'Vallida!' he screamed. 'Fight it! Fight the Voice! It is not you. You are Vallida. I love you . . .'

Suddenly one of the garrar beasts swooped at him and a blow from the side of its claw knocked him senseless.

Negg and Millon watched the whole scene with amazement and horror. It seemed Bardek was dead and Vallida reclaimed.

Vallida turned away from them, and without even a glance at the fallen body of Bardek, walked off across the plain, her three familiars circling darkly above her head.

CHAPTER 7

Return to the Mountains

Bardek was not dead, but unconscious.

Negg and Millon squatted beside him silently for a long time, considering what to do. Their first reaction had been to leave him and find their way back to the marshlands, but they were not sure where the marshlands lay. Ahead of them the Kariva mountain range rose huge and mysterious. Its giant walls of rock could be shelter or prison. The two marsh dwellers looked at it with dread, but they knew that Bardek had a family and it would probably be to their advantage to keep him alive and take him home.

They made a kind of make-shift hammock out of the girl's discarded cloak, rolled him over on to it, and carried him between them. His weight stretched the fabric to its limit and their arms began to ache. They had to stop a great many times to rest, and it seemed that the mountains that looked so near were retreating from them as they struggled towards them. What had appeared a solid wall of rock now revealed itself to be a series of jagged ridges, one behind the other, dauntingly high to their weary limbs and thirsty throats. They looked back to the plains. The city was a tiny smudge on the horizon and seemed to be detached from the land, floating in a strange haze, the plains between immense. Bardek had led them, knowing their safest route. But they had learned enough in their short experience of the desert to know that, although the plains appeared flat and featureless from a distance and offered no obstruction to the gaze from one end to the other, there were many places where movements of rock or the strange flash floods that had washed Bardek to them had caused great pits and troughs. Sometimes, even when the sand looked firm and flat, it could give way under their feet without warning.

It seemed to them that the whole adventure had turned sour, and they did not look forward to facing Bardek's questions as to why they had not pursued the girl and brought her back. The only excuse they could think of was that she had seemed to be willing to go. They had watched her for a long time and she had not once looked back.

Exhausted and hot they at last reached the huge boulders that lay strewn at the base of the first steep rock face and stared gloomily at the formidable heights. Some of the scree looked smooth and slippery, and they could see that one false move could bring the whole mountainside sliding down. They would have to climb the firm but precipitous rock cliffs further to the south.

The dry and crackling sand had given way to fertile soil as they approached the mountains, and in the shadow of a vast boulder they rested on the soft, thick leaves of plants. They were so hungry they ate anything they could find that looked edible, the sour sharp taste of the desert prickle-bushes that they had been living on driven out at last by the sweet red leaves of flowering bush and the fleshy nuts of a small ground hugging plant.

Negg cried out with joy when he caught the faint sound of water dripping and, following it, found a small gully where a waterfall dropped like a thin silver sword from a series of ledges into a dark pool. The pool had no stream running from it, its depths were buried in the mountain, but they bathed and drank, light-headed with relief that they had at last reached water, food and shelter.

Bardek had opened his eyes several times, but had not been conscious enough to question what was happening. They laid him in the shade beside the pool and splashed water on his face.

At last he shook himself free of the clinging lethargy that

had beset him since the garrar claw had struck, and pulled himself up to a sitting position, but it was a few moments before he remembered Vallida. Millon and Negg watched him sympathetically, but warily. They did not want to be led straight back over that desolate plain again. They could see the dawning of his anxiety for her and looked at each other uneasily.

'She went back,' Negg said in answer to the question in Bardek's eyes. 'There was nothing we could do about it.'

Bardek struggled to rise, but fell weakly back again.

'She went willingly,' Millon said hastily. 'They didn't touch her.'

'They couldn't have been real garrar beasts,' Negg added, 'or we'd be dead. They were flying right over her and didn't once attack her.'

Bardek buried his head in his hands. The marsh dwellers stood beside him awkwardly, not knowing what to do or say. It seemed a long time before he looked up again. When he did he gazed back across the plain towards Bar-geda. But he knew that he was too weak now to return and dare again what he had dared before. Half formed thoughts swam into his mind. He had been brought up to believe that the priests of the Temple of the White Star were not only the most powerful force in the community but also the guardians of all that was Good and Right. Yet he had seen how they treated Vallida, and now it seemed they used garrar beasts as their familiars. His feelings for the girl were so strong it was not possible for him to forget her. He could not bear to think of her used and abused by disembodied Beings, and would do everything in his power to smash the crystal Skull into a million fragments. Strange that when he first saw the Skull he had thought it beautiful. He remembered how moved he had been gazing into the 'universe' that appeared to be contained within its cranium. The memory teased him. He felt that somewhere in that memory lay hidden a key that he would need, but his head was hurting and his mind confused.

'We think,' Negg cut across his thought, 'that we should take you home to your family and that when you are fit and we're better prepared we should make another attempt to set her free.' Bardek knew that he had to accept this, although it was more than likely that the priesthood would also be better prepared.

Firilla and Glidd came to his mind, and he was ashamed how rarely he had thought of them since he left home. Now he felt a longing for the quiet simplicity of the life he had known with them, smarting to think how often he had resented their making his decisions for him, wishing now that they could tell him what to do. But he knew that he had passed the point in his life where he could ask others to decide for him. He was alone until his death and master of his own destiny. 'Yes,' he thought with sudden clarity, 'master, not slave to man or Star!'

When he had eaten the leaves and nuts they had gathered and drunk the cold water of the pool, they helped him to his feet and, leaning on Negg, he made an attempt to walk. Their progress was slow, but gradually they climbed the mountain, veering always to the north, where Bardek's home was.

When they were near enough for Bardek to feel they might come across Glidd out hunting, he asked them to stop for a while. He wanted to be well rested when he faced his family for the first time since his adventure, knowing that the reunion would not be easy. He knew that he had changed a great deal since he had left home and didn't want to be trapped again in Firilla's image of him. He had shed it like a slither-snake its skin. Would she see the difference in him? Would she acknowledge his right to change? And there was one more thing . . .

'I think,' he said hesitatingly to his companions, 'we should not tell my family about Vallida and the Temple.'

They looked at him questioningly.

'What we did would be considered by them to be great sacrilege. My mother in particular wouldn't understand.'

Negg shrugged. 'It never happened,' he said cheerfully.

'Millon?'

'Anything you say, my friend. It is your family. You know them.'

'I can tell them about the flood on the plain and the marshes and all that happened there, but not . . . but not what we did at the Temple.' Negg and Millon nodded. They were already finding it difficult to believe it had really happened and would have no problem in treating it like a dream. But Bardek recalled every detail now, and they burned in his heart like fire.

'How did you get to the marshes?' Negg asked curiously.

'I don't know. Someone must have found me after the flood and taken me home to recover . . . which goes to show that not all marsh people are as callous as some would like to make out.'

'Whoever it was probably thought he would get a good ransom for . . .' Negg was saying when he was interrupted by a sound from above them. They looked up to see a bowman standing on a rock watching them, his arrow drawn.

Bardek waved energetically.

'Glidd!' he shouted. 'Glidd! It's me! I've come home.'

The bowman looked hard at Bardek but did not lower his bow. The voice that had risen to him was thin with distance and he could not be sure that it was the one he so longed to hear.

He waited, watching them tensely as they toiled up the track. At last they were near enough for Glidd to see that it was indeed Bardek. He slung his bow to his back and jumped off the rock, running and leaping towards them, shouting with delight, disregarding the stones that were slipping from beneath his feet and which could at any moment have sent him to his death on the rocks below.

Bardek struggled towards him full of joy, but too weak to go far. Negg held him back and the three of them waited on a ledge. When at last Glidd reached them the marsh dwellers were ignored as Bardek and Glidd flung their arms around each other, almost weeping with relief to be together again.

Negg looked at Millon and raised his eyebrows. Such showing of emotion was embarrassing to them. Millon shrugged and they both turned their backs and began to throw small stones at a target, until at last Bardek remembered them and introduced them to Glidd.

As they climbed, Glidd warned Bardek that Firilla had taken his disappearance very hard and in some ways blamed Glidd himself for it. 'You'll see a great change in her,' he said sadly. 'She has aged.'

'I left a message.' Bardek said, trying not to feel guilty. 'I thought she would understand . . .'

'Message?'

'I wrote on the ground with a garrar quill and put my red scarf with it so you would find it easily.'

'The storm must have washed it away. I found only the crown of garrar feathers,' and here he looked hard at Bardek, 'and the scarf which was half way down the mountain as though you had fallen.'

'Oh,' sighed Bardek. 'How she must have worried.' He hurried forward, leaving the others to follow more slowly.

He found Firilla tending her garden. Her back was to him but he was shocked to see how thin she had grown. He called to her and she turned, her face pale and drawn. She moved slowly, staring at him, holding herself back, afraid to react until she was sure that he was not once again an insubstantial vision.

It was only when he walked forward with his arms out to her, the bruising from the garrar claw at the side of his head still visible, his clothes shabby and dusty from all he had been through, that she allowed herself to accept that he was really there as solid as the day he had left.

She did not move forward but, like a flower opening, life and strength seemed to unfold in her. Her back straightened, her eyes cleared, her smile spread like the light of the White Star at dawn. He took her in his arms and held her close.

'I'm sorry,' he whispered. 'I'm so sorry.' He rocked her back and forth as though she were the child and he the parent. Their relationship had subtly changed and she knew that she could never again command him, nor keep him with her if he did not want to stay. Afraid, she looked into his eyes, but great love and warmth was there. A flicker of hope that he had not yet paid homage to the Lord of the Dark Star grew in her heart.

She looked over his shoulder to Glidd whom she had wronged. He was standing awkwardly at the entrance to her garden, looking at her with eyes shining at her pleasure, two strangers behind him. They looked at each other long and deeply for the first time since Bardek had disappeared and words could not have expressed what passed between them.

She released herself from Bardek's hold and ran to Glidd, weeping, clinging to him, kissing him, asking his pardon.

Negg and Millon began to wonder if they would not have been better off on the inhospitable plain or amongst the dangers of the city. What kind of people were these that they wept so easily and flung themselves upon each other with such abandon at the slightest opportunity?

Bardek caught their expressions and laughed. Joyfully he led them to his mother's house and set about finding them food, occasionally looking out of the window to smile with pleasure at Glidd and Firilla, who were still standing where he had left them, locked in each other's arms, talking as though they would never catch up with all they wanted to say to each other.

At last they came arm in arm into the house, and then it was his turn to talk and tell tales.

At first Firilla was so happy to see Bardek again she welcomed his friends warmly, but when it emerged in the telling that in spite of their red bowman's clothes they were marsh dwellers born under the Dark Star, her fear and her hostility began to embarrass her son. Negg and Millon at once insisted on leaving, saying that they would find somewhere else to sleep in the mountains before they returned to the marshes. Bardek protested, but his mother was so determined to get them out of her house and out of her son's life that she accepted their offer in a way that made it impossible for them to stay.

Glidd went with them and helped them to build a little hut just beyond Firilla's garden. With his friendliness he made up for Firilla's hostility, spending some time with them while they settled in, interested in everything they had to say about themselves and their lives in the marshes.

When at last he left them he sat for a long while by himself, thinking over their conversation. He saw no reason to believe they were evil just because tradition said they were. His doubts about the justice of the Star caste system rose to the surface again.

CHAPTER 8

Nea

The High Priestess of the Temple of the Blue Star, Maya, paced the hall of mirror-stones when she should have been sleeping. A hundred images of herself paced with her, turning when she turned, stopping when she stopped. She had seen that there was something wrong at the temple of white crystal, but when she sent to enquire, her messenger reported that she was mistaken, that there was nothing wrong.

'Did you see nothing different about the temple?'

'Nothing, my lady.'

'Was the light not subtly different?'

'It was the same as always, my lady.'

Maya's beautiful eyes clouded, and the young messenger before her looked uneasy.

'What should I have seen, my lady?'

'You should have seen exactly what you did see, child.'

The messenger looked puzzled. To her, as to anyone else on Agaron, it was unthinkable that anything should be 'different' in the Temple of the White Star. The questions of the High Priestess were disturbing, implying as they did that it was possible for something to change, something to be amiss.

Maya saw the anxiety in the young girl's eyes and spoke soothingly. 'Forget that I have asked you these questions,' she said. 'A shadow passed over my own heart, and I saw it over the whole town.' She looked thoughtfully at the girl, her intense blue eyes searching her face. The novice shifted her weight from foot to foot, wondering what the priestess was thinking.

'Come with me.' The High Priestess broke the silence at last, turning on her silver sandaled heel and beckoning to her companion.

She led the girl through corridor after corridor of subtly shaded blue crystal, where sometimes the walls were so clear they felt they were in a vast hall, the constricting walls of the passage almost invisible. At other times the rock was flawed and murky and they seemed to be swimming through an underwater tunnel that was at every moment growing narrower. Sometimes they passed doors and heard from behind them the fine tinkling of music, or a voice raised in litany. But as they walked further and further, the frequency of rooms and doors and sounds, the chance of meeting other people, grew less.

They came at last to the legendary Court of the Fountains the girl had heard about but never seen. The door, made from one vast slab of turquoise, opened as Maya laid a slender finger lightly on it.

As she entered the hall the girl gasped. It was roofed with slabs of crystal alternately transparent and opaque, and light came shafting from above, each shaft brilliant with a myriad glinting specks of what looked like fine gold dust. Seven fountains were in the hall, each spouting from the centre of a circular bowl finely wrought in silver. Smooth and shallow steps of stone in different shades of blue led up to each bowl. The waters that rose almost to the ceiling and fell again made lovely music, each note harmonizing with the rest. Around the sides of the hall were huge silver urns from which grew plants in such profusion that once inside the hall one seemed more in a forest than a room, the plants heavy with glowing blooms looming out of the only dimness in the hall. The floor was covered with gold dust, which formed drifts in some places against the edges of the raised fountains.

Maya slipped a fine-meshed gold veil over her head as they entered so that she did not breath the gold dust in, but the girl was left unprotected. The High Priestess turned to the girl. 'Take off your clothes,' she said coolly.

Alarmed, the girl obeyed, silk falling from her limbs like mist from a valley when the White Star seeks it out. When she stood naked, the Priestess pointed to the vast fluted silver bowl that held one of the fountains in its gleaming cup. Trembling and confused the girl mounted the steps to the lip of the great bowl.

'What is to be your priest-name, girl?'

The girl hesitated: was she to be priested here and now, without the others? The voice of the High Priestess was so commanding, her eye so piercing, that she knew she could not refuse to tell her, though she had been forbidden to use the priest-name before she was priested.

'A-ha-yi,' she said so softly that none but Maya's trained ears would have caught it.

The High Priestess pointed her finger at the water. Fearfully the girl climbed on to the lip of the bowl. 'And your birth name?'

'Nea.'

The Priestess came up the steps behind her and Nea could feel her closeness like a touch. 'A-ha-yi and Nea both,' Maya said in a voice that seemed to echo in the girl's head. 'Know that you are bound to silence on what has passed between us and what will pass between us.'

She placed her hand on Nea's back. The girl found herself propelled forward by the strong but almost imperceptible pressure of the older woman's hand. Her body slipped into the cool water and, as she sank to the bottom, the flashing webs of light that were the reflection of the water moving against the fluted silver sides enclosed her and rippled over her skin. She rose to the surface, but the force of the central fountain breaking on her head drove her down to the bottom of the bowl again.

The beauty of the flickering silver light, the smooth coolness of the water on her bare skin, gave her a sensation of ecstasy. She turned and turned, driving herself through the liquid with movements of sinuous grace. Above her Maya stood, watching.

But at last Nea needed air and swam to the surface, only to be driven down again by the pressure of the falling water. She began to feel dizzy and frightened, longing for air. The beauty had become menacing, the sensation of pleasure, pain.

She looked up desperately and saw through the water the image of the High Priestess looking down at her from the silver rim, broken into scattered fragments of sapphire blue and brittle gold.

Terror suddenly gripped her heart. What if the lady meant her to die? She had thought of death only as a word, and now it had presence and reached for her . . . for *her!*

She struggled to the surface. The water, disturbed by the thrashing of her limbs, became a whirling kaleidoscope of blue and silver and gold. In that moment of confusion it seemed to her that her whole life had always been no more than a sparkle of such fragments in motion. Would leaving it be such a loss? But after the confusion came clarity, and the will to live, on whatever terms, under any conditions. She fought to reach the air, her lungs aching, her heart pounding. And then with horror she noticed the bright sparkles of light going out, one by one, and felt herself sinking into darkness.

Maya, watching her fall, touched a switch. The fountain gave a sigh, and ceased. Swiftly, the High Priestess stepped into the pool, took the limp figure of the girl in her arms and lifted her out.

Later, Nea was found lying on the marble floor of the Court of the Fountains, fully clothed. When she was roused she could remember nothing of what had occurred or how she had found her way there. She was taken before the High Priestess for disciplining, for it was against the Law to enter the Court before initiation.

'Were you alone?' Maya asked, looking at her closely.

The girl shook her head, bewildered. 'I must have been, my lady, though I can't remember.' Something teased at the back of her mind, but she could give it no form.

'What did you hope to do there?'

Nea remained silent.

'Was there an oath you wished to take?'

'I don't know my lady.'

The girl looked so miserable and confused Maya was satisfied that she could remember nothing. She was pleased. She wanted no rumours spread that the High Priestess of the Blue Star suspected that something was wrong at the Temple of the White Star. The whole stability of the community of colonists on Agaron depended on the confidence the people had in the Star Temple system. Change could be allowed in minor things, but never in anything to do with the Temples. That her own heart had started to question was bad enough, but that anyone else should would be disastrous.

The girl Nea was told that because she had trespassed in the hall she would not be allowed to take her final vows as priestess for another full cycle of the Seven Stars. Meanwhile, she was to attend the Lady Maya in her private chambers. There she was told that her duties would be to bathe and massage her Mistress, robe her for ceremonial occasions and, at the time of rest, share her bed.

CHAPTER 9

The Cage of Pearls

Bardek had not intended his mother or Glidd to know anything of his adventures at the Temple, but as time went by
and he and his two friends stayed on the mountain preparing
for their second attempt to rescue Vallida, first Glidd, and
then Firilla, found out about it. While Glidd was worried,
Firilla was angry. She had grown accustomed to the presence of Negg and Millon and after a while had accepted
them as friends of her son, forgetting that they had anything
to do with the much feared Dark Star. But prejudices die
hard, and when Bardek let slip something of what they had
done, and were preparing to try again, she blamed it all on
Negg and Millon.

'Such people always cause trouble. They have no sense
of what is right and proper.'

'But mother, it was not their idea. It was mine. They helped
me. They saved my life!'

'Nonsense. No one of the Red Star would think of committing such a sacrilege!'

'Am I of the Red Star?' he asked pointedly.

'Of course you are!' she snapped.

'Mother?' He looked at her close and hard. She began to
look uncomfortable and turned away from him.

'Why do you question it?' she asked, a catch in her voice.

'Because I was told by the Seer woman in the marshes
that I was one of them, and later in the Hall of the Skull, and
on the plains, I was called "Child of the Dark Star".'

'That was because you were with those people. They
thought you were one of them.'

'No, I don't think so.'

'Do you doubt me?'

'I don't doubt that you love me, but sometimes . . . I think that you don't know what's best for me.'

She rounded on him, passionately angry. 'You were born under the Red Star, like Glidd. You are a bowman by training and by nature. Never doubt it!'

He shrugged. 'I believe you . . . but . . .'

'No. There must be no "buts"!'

'Why have you tried to keep me away from other people?'

'I don't try to keep you away from other people. Our home is here in the mountains, that's all.'

'Then when I say I must move to the city now that I am grown, you will have no objection?'

She bit her lip. Bardek could see what he was doing to her, and with his newfound knowledge of the outside world thought he knew why. 'Mother,' he said gently, 'what must be, must be. I have been chosen to save Vallida.'

'She was chosen by the gods to be the Oracle! The punishment for tampering with the will of the gods will be more terrible than anything she has yet endured. You will not help her by interfering. Her punishment will be greater than yours for she is a Chosen One, whereas you, for all you say, are not Chosen. It was you who sought the Temple and decided to interfere, and for this I blame your head-strong youth and bad companions.'

'When will you understand? I hadn't even met Negg and Millon when I decided to rescue her from the Temple.'

'The punishment will be entirely yours then,' she said in despair.

'There will be no punishment. The Voices that speak through the Oracle are false. Agaron will be the better for being rid of them.'

'How do you know that they are false?'

'She says . . .'

'She says,' Firilla almost screamed. 'You're bewitched!

If she told you to jump in a pit of fire you would do it!'

'No. I wouldn't,' he said thoughtfully, 'unless my own wits told me it was the right thing to do.'

'Your own wits! Don't you see how difficult it is to tell when you're using your own wits and when you're being manipulated? You fought three garrar beasts and yet you tell me now they were not what they seemed.'

His face was grave. What she said was true, but he was not prepared to stop thinking for himself just because sometimes he had been proved wrong. 'Each thing that has happened to me has taught me something,' he said after a long pause. 'I'll not be so easily deceived again.'

Firilla burst into tears. 'You're determined to destroy yourself!'

'No, mother, I'm determined to save us all from something I feel deep inside me to be evil.'

'What do you know of good and evil, you child of the Dark Lord!' she screamed, beside herself with frustration and despair, not realizing what she was saying.

Bardek looked at her, stunned. It was now no longer possible to hide from the shadow of his birth. He turned on his heel and walked away.

He walked and walked, hardly knowing where he was going, his thoughts like dark leaves in a storm. He would not return until he had proved within himself, once and for all, the truth or the falsehood of the Star Law of Agaron.

When Bardek did not return at the time for food and sleep, they all guessed that he must have gone back to Bar-geda. Glidd's face was grave as he looked at Negg and Millon, but he found theirs cheerful and excited. The novelty of being in the mountains had worn off, and they were growing impatient with the inactivity. Bardek and Glidd hunted their meat, Firilla's garden provided the vegetables. The marsh dwellers, accustomed to a constant challenge, a constant danger, were bored with safety. They volunteered at once to go after him.

It seemed Firilla had stormed herself out, for she was very pale and quiet. She prepared food and drinks for the marsh dwellers and for Bardek in case they caught up with him, and wished them well with such graciousness that it was clear she had come to terms with who they were.

'Look after him,' she said to them in a voice that barely disguised the emotion she was feeling. But she did not weep, and Negg was glad of that.

'He will have two extra shadows!' Negg promised, grinning at her so cheerfully and confidently that she could not help feeling less anxious.

'But be careful,' she said, this time including them in her concern.

Negg made a fist and shook it at the sky. 'Let the Stars themselves be careful! Negg of the Py-yetti is coming!'

She saw how strong he was, how eager for adventure, and she knew that Bardek was lucky, after all, to have him for a friend. 'Hurry,' she said. 'Leave the boasting until later!'

Negg laughed and shouldered the pack she had prepared.

Glidd went with them to the edge of the plains, but then returned to Firilla. He found her packing food and clothes. 'What are you doing?' he asked in astonishment.

'You and I are going to Bar-geda,' she said calmly.

'No we're not!' he said sharply.

'I am going even if you are not,' she insisted. 'I can't stay here and wait hopelessly for what will happen. I have thought of a way I might be able to help.'

He took her in his arms. 'My love. I know how you feel, but we can no longer live his life for him. Who knows but this may be his destiny?'

'Who knows but this may be *my* destiny!' she said defiantly.

'I can't let you do this. He wouldn't wish it.'

'He needn't know.'

'We might make things worse for him.'

'I can help. I know it!' Her pale face was set and firm. He had had experience of her stubbornness before and knew that she would not be diverted from her decision. He sighed. 'How can you help?' he asked, but she could tell from the tone of his voice that his resistance was weakening.

'I am a mother. I have a way.'

'Tell me.'

'I'll tell you when we reach Bar-geda.'

'I'll not take you!'

'I have said I will go alone.'

He knew that he was defeated and that he would go with her and do what he could to protect her.

Bardek reached the Temple of the White Star and found it as he had first seen it, perfect and complete, as though nothing had ever challenged or disturbed it. He warily circled it, deciding not to try to enter where he had before in case he was expected.

It was the time of the Red Star. 'A good time for ventures such as this,' he thought, for under the Red Star aggression and courage were at their peak. But even so he was so nervous that he twice jumped as a shadow seemed to move. He smiled ruefully, remembering how Glidd and he had often teased Firilla about her nervousness. For a moment he regretted causing her more anxiety, but when he thought how she had deceived him about his birth Star, he put his regrets aside.

He crouched, concentrating his thoughts on one face of the crystal wall as he had done before. But this time a violent spasm of pain passed through his temples, leaving a dull throbbing ache behind his eyes. He tried to hold concentration, but it was impossible. He opened his eyes hoping he would be through the wall, but he was not. He tried again, and again he suffered and retreated. He was sure this was some defensive work of the priests and was determined to break through it. He tried again.

This time, knowing the pain was inevitable, he forced himself by a deliberate act of will to accept it, to meet it as he would the challenge of a difficult cliff face to be climbed in the mountains. He focussed his awareness on the crystal and imagined himself moving forward. At the moment he 'touched' the wall a hundred thousand splinters of shattered crystal seemed to penetrate his skin and as many needles of light came rushing towards his eyes. But this time he refused to shrink back. He forced himself on and as he did so the pain eased and the physical sensation of splinters in his flesh gave way to a kind of numbness, the sharp onslaught of light fading to a steady glow. He found himself, exhausted and almost unconscious, lying on the floor within the building

He lay still for what seemed a long while, trying to summon the strength to move. When he finally managed it he found that the pain had returned and that every movement needed courage. He tried to stand up, but found the effort too much. He began to crawl across the hall towards the corridors that led deeper into the building.

He encountered no one, but the time he took to traverse each crystal tunnel was stretched out almost beyond endurance. The pain was so great that there were times when he would have given anything to have turned back, but he knew the way back was as difficult as the way forward, and he was not sure he would be able to summon the extra strength needed to break out again.

He tried not to think of what would happen if, when he found Vallida, he didn't have the strength to rescue her. Remembering his lesson from the marsh Seer, he tried to hold the image of her in his mind, not as he had seen her a prisoner in the crystal, but as she was when he put the cloak on her. The feeling he had had then as he touched her skin sustained him through a long and grueling journey to the centre of the Temple, his nerve as taut to the expectation of discovery as his body ached to the constant pain.

At last he found her. Again she was at the centre of a vast glimmering hall, but this time her cage was different. There was no crystal holding her immobile, no solidified light to be dissolved to set her free. Instead, a fine string of pearls held her silver hair in place and wound down her body, separating her breasts, binding the white silk of her clothes close to her flesh. From the cord of pearls around her waist other strings radiated outwards across the hall to join mysteriously into the crystal walls. Some threads of pearl ran along the floor, others hung, curving gently, a little above. So white and fine was she that she seemed a pearl herself, at the centre of a web of pearls.

She did not see him at first, and he watched her, too weak to move, his heart aching as he saw the droop of her head and shoulders, the sadness and the hopelessness of the expression on her face. He tapped the wall and she looked up, her face flooding with joy at the sight of him. But almost at once fear took its place and she shook her head, and raised her hand to warn him back.

He hesitated. The web of tiny shining pearls seemed frail enough, surely it would be easy to snap her free. In fact it so enhanced her beauty that desire for her began to bring strength back to his limbs.

'You must not touch the pearls,' she called, as loudly as she dared, but still so softly that her words barely reached him. He wondered if a giant spider-hag was lurking somewhere to attack him if he were to touch the web. He strained forward to see as far as he could into the hall, but there was nothing there besides Vallida and the fine threads of shining white. 'You can't reach me,' she said. 'Please leave me. If you touch the pearls you will die. They are charged with kill-power.'

'You are touching them . . .'

She shook her head sadly. 'They'll not let me die, although I long for death.'

'I'll take you out,' he said, more boldly than he felt. 'And this time I'll not let you go.'

'You have your bow with you. Put an arrow to my heart. That's the only way you can help me. I will not be used again.'

He felt as he had the first time when her thoughts were in his head, and experienced the revulsion she felt at the shapeless energies that used her body for their own purposes. No physical rape could be so shameful or so destructive.

'I will take you out,' he said, gritting his teeth and moving forward until he almost touched the threads.

'No!' she cried. 'I beg of you! I'll not see you die so cruelly.'

He paused. If what she said about the pearls was true, he would serve no purpose by seizing them. He would die and would not help her, and she would have the added suffering of seeing him destroyed and all her hope lost forever. He must think. Somehow, through the pain, he had to think. He realized the priests had been extremely cunning with this device. By tying the pearls around her in such a way as to make the beauty of her figure irresistible, they would lure him on. By weakening him with pain, he had to crawl and not touch the pearls on the floor or immediately above it. If only he could bring himself to stand upright he would be able to step over them.

He withdrew into the corridor so that she would not witness his struggle. Time and again he dragged himself up only to fall again as a wave of the pain overwhelmed him. Once or twice, momentarily, he fainted, but at last, clinging to the wall, he got to his feet. When Vallida saw him again he was standing, dragging step by step into the hall. She tried to hold her tears back, her heart crying out for help, not to the Stars that ruled Agaron, for she did not trust them, but blindly, hoping that somewhere in the universe there might be One who was greater than the Stars, more powerful than the Voices who ruled her planet.

Step by step Bardek moved forward. At the first thread of pearls he pulled his legs up one by one with his hands to cross over the slender deadly barrier. His limbs felt as heavy as weary-stone. Shaking with the effort, he rested, then tried again. With each success he seemed to gain strength until at last he stood before her, almost free of pain.

She saw him reaching for her and cried out. In his relief to be so near her he would have undone all his work by touching the threads about her body. Just in time he held back, though the strain of doing so was almost unbearable.

'Is there a way to break the thread without touching it?'

She shook her head.

'There must be. How do the priests release you when they come to fetch you?'

She puckered her forehead, thinking. 'They speak a word.'

'What word do they use? Think.'

She shook her head desperately. 'I don't know. I don't know,' she cried. 'I don't understand it.'

'You must hear it.'

'Yes, but I don't . . .'

'Remember the sound. It doesn't matter about the meaning. Sound is vibration. Vibrations cause movement. The movement the sound makes could shake the pearls free.'

She was sobbing.

'Think!' he shouted impatiently.

She could not think. Fear of the failure of his attempt to rescue her filled her mind. Despair and hopelessness dulled her wits.

Bardek began to shout — yelling at the top of his voice every sound he could think of, every combination of sound . . . surely in that furious medley one would be the key. The girl wept. The pearls rose and fell on her breast with her sobs. He did not care who heard him, who came to find him there. He did not want to live without her. In the cadences of the meaningless sounds he uttered, his passionate love for her rang out . . .

Suddenly the pearls slid from her body, the silk of her dress was freed, her silver hair fell shining to her back. He seized her in his arms, lifted her and ran, leaping over the fallen threads that lay in disorder on the floor, escaping from the hall just before the individual pearls coiled loose and, shimmering, covered the white crystal tiles completely.

The sound of his cry of joy rang like a bell, gaining

strength with every echo, down the corridors of the gleaming building.

When Firilla and Glidd reached the city, the Red Star was high and Firilla's courage was at its greatest. She told him quite boldly of her plan. 'I am Bardek's mother and however much I may disapprove of what he is doing, my love for him will always make me help him and protect him in any way I can. Vallida has a mother too and that mother, if she knew how much her daughter was suffering, would be bound to try to help her.'

It was known that the mother of the Oracle was always the High Priestess of the Temple of the Blue Star, so it was to the Blue Temple that Firilla was determined they should go. During the time of the Blue Star it was never possible to approach the Blue Temple, for the rituals were immensely important and completely secret. But during the ascendancy of the other Stars, petitioners were admitted, provided that they were female, for no male was ever allowed to cross the threshold of the Blue Temple.

Without hesitation Firilla made straight for the Blue Temple and asked the gatekeeper for permission to enter as a petitioner. Glidd was forced to wait outside the main gate in a small paved court. He paced backwards and forwards impatiently, full of misgivings that the high Priestess, whose child had been taken from her before she saw it, would have any of the deep maternal love that Firilla was relying on.

Inside the anteroom of the Hall of Petitioners, Firilla sat among other women and waited for her turn to speak. As she moved nearer and nearer to the moment when she would be brought before the High Priestess, she began to feel more and more nervous. If she could prevent Bardek entering the Temple of the White Star before he had the support of the High Priestess of the Blue Temple, Vallida might be helped with only minimum damage to the ancient mysteries, and her son might one day thank her for her intervention. But if he had already entered the forbidden place and she could not enlist the help of the High Priestess, she might well be bringing about his death.

She shut her eyes, appalled at the responsibility she had taken upon herself. Should she leave now before her turn to speak arrived? But it was already too late.

Suddenly, trembling with apprehension, she was admitted to the inner audience chamber. She was led, feeling small and insignificant, between two rows of immensely tall columns that held up the shining ceiling. Priestesses in ribbons and feathers walked casually among the colonnades on either side, taking no notice of her, and on a throne raised on a flight of steps of exquisitely veined marble at the far end of the huge hall sat the High Priestess herself.

As Firilla drew nearer, her heart sank. The great lady sat straight and stiff, her gown of ribbons falling around her on the throne, revealing parts of her body Firilla thought it immodest to show. Beside her stood a girl, naked except for a few ribbons tied loosely round her waist and falling to her knees. She held a fan with which she occasionally fanned the priestess, but which she never once used to cover her nakedness.

Firilla swallowed and wondered if there were not some other petition she could hastily invent, for the one burning in her heart seemed more and more inappropriate. But Bardek's danger was great and the pity he had aroused in her for Vallida drove her forward until she fell at last onto her knees at the foot of the throne, almost fainting with fear at what she was proposing to do.

She was in fact silent so long that the chamberlain who had brought her in gave her a push with her foot. At this Firilla looked up, startled to see that the woman appeared to be hovering in the air above her. The ceiling was made of such polished stone the whole hall was reflected in it and she seemed to be floating between two realities, two images of herself. She took a deep breath. Win or lose, she would have to play the gamble through.

She raised herself and spoke as loudly and as clearly as she could. 'My lady, this plea is so personal, I appeal to you to hear it privately.'

Bored by the endless trivial petitions the High Priestess usually had to deal with, the women around the hall pricked up their ears at this and moved closer. Firilla flushed, but held her ground. 'I beg you hear me, my lady. If, then, you wish to make what I say known to those here, I'll gladly repeat it.'

The High Priestess's eyes sparked with interest. She raised her hand and indicated that Firilla could approach closer. The other priestesses tried to move closer too but she waved them back imperiously.

When Firilla was only a few steps away from the great lady she knelt again, but looked enquiringly at the naked girl. The lady Maya smiled briefly. 'She has my confidence. You may speak freely with her present.'

Firilla hesitated. The girl had a bold, sensual look, and was eyeing her distastefully. She could not say what she had to say in front of her. 'My lady . . . I cannot . . .'

Maya looked into Firilla's eyes. There was such distress, such sincerity there, that she was impressed. She turned to the girl.

'Leave us,' she said gently. Nea pouted and looked as though she would stay, but a dangerous glint came to Maya's eyes and she decided not to risk her displeasure. She took her time leaving, but she left. Maya's eyes followed the girl as she walked the length of the hall, her hungry gaze caressing her every step of the way, Nea aware of it, and with every movement of her supple body, encouraging it. Only when she was out of sight did the High Priestess turn her attention to Firilla.

'And now . . . this "personal" matter?' she said, a hint of impatience in her voice.

'My lady . . .' Firilla was trembling, but she had gone too far to stop now.

'What is it? I cannot let you take up my time unless you speak and speak of something indeed too personal to be heard by anyone but the two of us.'

'My lady . . . it is . . . about your daughter.'

The woman's mask-like face showed visible signs of shock behind its gold paint. 'Careful . . .' she hissed.

Firilla plunged on, knowing that there was no going back. 'I . . . I don't know if you know or not . . . but . . . your daughter . . . the . . . the Oracle . . . is suffering great hardship. I . . . I thought perhaps you did not know . . . otherwise you would not have allowed it . . .'

Firilla was scarlet and sweating profusely. Her voice seemed loud and hollow in the great hall, but no one heard her but the Lady Maya, whose eyes bored into hers. 'You risk much in speaking of this to me.'

'I . . . I know. But I thought . . . you ought to know . . .'

'And how do you know this when I, the High Priestess of the planet Agaron, do not?'

Firilla shook her head helplessly.

'I cannot tell you that, my lady, but surely even if you do not believe me . . . you will send to see if it is true.'

'And what shall I do with you who have knowledge that is forbidden.'

Firilla spread her hands. She was near to fainting. 'As you please, my lady . . .' she whispered in a dry voice.

'I will keep you here. You will never see the light again if you have lied.'

'I have not lied, my lady.'

'We will see.' There was a pause. 'Take her to my private cell,' Maya called out suddenly, and several novices ran forward to seize Firilla and lead her away. Weeping and exhausted, not knowing if she had done the right thing or not, she was pushed into a small cold room and left alone.

Bardek fled through the corridors of white crystal with Vallida in his arms, pursued by the echoes of the sounds he had made to free her. Where is the skull?' he cried. 'We must destroy it this time!'

They began to hear footsteps other than their own running through the corridors. The priests had found their Oracle missing and were in pursuit.

'Put me down,' Vallida said. 'I will lead you.'

He stopped running long enough for her to slide from his arms and hand in hand they ran and slid and ran, purposefully now, for the girl knew her way to the Hall of the Skull.

They rounded a corner and almost ran straight into a group of priests.

It was Vallida who managed to stop in time and turn Bardek round and pull him after her as she fled. That way was blocked, but she knew of another. The Temple was full of confusing noises. Not only were the echoes of Bardek still going round and round but the sounds of running footsteps had developed echoes too, and it became impossible for them to judge which were new sounds and which were echoes. Pursuers seemed to be coming at them from all sides, but at last they broke into the Hall of the Skull — and slid to a halt, amazed at what they saw.

On the right hand side of the Skull was the High Priest of the Temple of the White Star. On the left hand side of the Skull was the High Priestess of the Temple of the Blue Star.

Maya, looking at the two figures that had come bursting so unceremoniously into the sacred place, saw a young man, bronzed and clad in red leather, his arms bare but for a bracelet, his jerkin open to the waist. And with him a girl like quicksilver and gossamer, clinging to his arm.

Her daughter!

Her heart skipped a beat.

'My Lord High Priest, what is this?' she said coldly.

Behind the young couple other priests came rushing in ready to seize them, but as soon as they saw the Lady, they paused, uncertain what to do.

'This young bowman,' the High Priest said steadily, 'has made two attempts to steal our Oracle. The first time we were lenient with him. This time he will die.'

'No!' cried Vallida. 'No. Kill me! Punish me! He has done

'nothing but answer my call for help.'

'And why should you call for help, girl?' the Lady said carefully.

'No reason at all,' the High Priest interrupted. 'He has bewitched her with his body, and distracted her from her duties.'

'Please,' cried Vallida. 'Lady, hear me.'

'I already incur the wrath of the gods by coming here and looking upon you, girl. If you have anything to say . . .'

'She is held here as though she were no more than a vessel to be used by others,' said Bardek fiercely. 'Yet she is a living human being . . . she is lonely . . . she longs . . .'

'Are we not all lonely . . . do we not all long?'

'Not like this. Not like she does. Believe me . . .'

'Enough!' shouted the High Priest angrily. 'Seize him. And as for you, Lady . . .' he turned to the Blue Lady as the priests seized Bardek, 'the High Council shall hear of your visit to your daughter. You know the Law.'

It took three men to subdue Bardek, but they held him at last helpless between them. Vallida fell to her knees, weeping, such hopelessness and despair in her face that no one who looked at her could fail to be moved. Her mother saw that everything the young man had said was true.

She knew that the role of Oracle had never been an easy one, and that it was of great importance to the community and worth the sacrifice both she and her daughter had had to make, and yet . . . and yet the inrush of love she suddenly felt for the girl, and all the longings for escape she herself had felt in her beautiful domed prison, came together now to make her lose her sense of loyalty to the rigid system of Star Laws.

She turned abruptly, unexpectedly, and threw her full weight against the plinth on which the skull was resting.

Vallida twitched horribly as though she were a wooden doll pulled by strings. A fearsome voice issued from her distorted mouth.

'Woman, you profane the sacred mystery. Death will be

your reward and the horrors of dying will be all that you remember until the end of time!'

Using the slight edge this distraction gave him, Bardek, with a supreme effort, broke loose and flung himself towards the skull. The Priestess, seeing his intention, avoided the High Priest's hands and together they hurled their weight against the plinth.

Vallida gave a terrifying, horrible scream that was not her own.

The crystal skull rocked, settled, rocked again, then toppled from the plinth and fell, rolling towards the wall, hitting it with a sickening thud. As it struck, the whole building shook and cracked. The tall crystal towers shuddered, and began to splinter and fall.

Bardek saw Vallida standing in the middle of the hall, limp and expressionless. He seized her hand and pulled her after him through the hole the skull had made when it hit the wall.

Outside there was as much chaos as within. The whole hill was shaking and the ground moving under his feet. He heard a scream and looked back. Maya, the High Priestess, was falling in a cloud of crystal dust. He saw her twist and turn desperately to avoid a huge block of shattered wall. She was not quick enough.

Horrified, Bardek watched her crushed.

Vallida sank to the ground, her expression a complete blank. He looked at her in despair, shocked at her lack of feeling.

'Don't you care?' he shouted suddenly. 'Don't you care that your mother has been killed? Don't you care that all this is happening to free you . . .'

She looked at him as though he were a long, long way away and all that was happening around her had no reality for her.

How long would Bardek have stood there with the dust falling, and every moment the danger of being recaptured or being hit by falling debris increasing, had he not heard someone calling his name? He looked round to see Negg and Millon struggling towards him, shouting for him to move, waving and gesticulating. At the same time some of the priests who had managed to get free from the Temple were advancing through the dying remnants of the once beautiful garden. Negg and Millon moved to head them off as Bardek finally came to his senses and, lifting Vallida, carried her to the edge of the rock platform and then, half pushing, half holding her, clambered down the rugged slope.

CHAPTER 10

The Flight

In her cell, in the dark, Firilla could not judge the passing of time. Occasionally she heard a bell ring in the distance, the sound muffled by the walls, and once or twice she fancied she heard footsteps and flung herself against the stone, her ear pressed to it, straining to hear if they were approaching or retreating. But no one came.

After a while hunger and thirst tormented her, but then she almost forgot these sensations as her fear of the dark grew. As a child she had lived among open fields, and it was only when she had entered the forests of the tree-garths that she had felt what she was now feeling. She remembered the time when she had wandered further in search of forest fungi than she had intended. The tall, notched stems had crowded round her, the interweaving branches cutting out nearly all the light. Everywhere she turned seemed hostile, alien, menacing. Darkness was the medium of the Dark Lord. In darkness one was not safe even from one's own thoughts!

She began to scream and beat on the walls with her fists. Surely Glidd would be trying to free her. But how would he ever find her in this place? Tears streamed down her cheeks. She had born a child under the Dark Star and had kept him alive, and, as though this were not guilt enough, she had attempted to help him in tampering with the sacred mysteries of the White Star.

'O my Lady, goddess of the Green Star,' she sobbed. 'Forgive me and help me! Protect my son and prevent evil coming to him. Protect me and release me from this dark place.'

Suddenly, as though in answer to her prayer, light beamed in upon her. She reeled back, her hands over her red and smarting eyes. 'Glidd!' she cried.

'No, not Glidd,' a cold voice said.

Disappointed, Firilla retreated as far as she could into the corner, peeping through her fingers, trying to see through the painful glare. Gradually, as her eyes adjusted, she began to see the outline of the figure, and then, slowly, more detail. It was the girl who had stood next to the throne of the High Priestess. Firilla's heart leapt with joy. She was being sent for at last. Everything must be all right, for had the High Priestess not said that it was only if she had lied that she would never see the light again? She moved forward eagerly, but when she was fully in the light she stopped short. She could see the girl's face clearly, and it was filled with such malice and hate that it was disfigured almost beyond recognition.

Terrified, Firilla took a step back, but too late. The girl had lashed out, her long nails scoring across Firilla's cheeks, narrowly missing her eyes. She gasped with pain and covered her face with her hands.

The girl attacked again.

Firilla dodged as best she could, but in the confined space of the cell she had very little chance of escaping the ripping of the girl's long claw-like nails.

'What's happened?' Firilla managed to gasp out, as she ducked and dodged, stinging lines of pain gradually covering her whole body like a web, the girl having ripped aside her clothes and attacked her flesh. 'Why? Why?' Firilla sobbed.

'You sent her to her death! You knew it would happen! You are in the service of the Dark Lord! You will pay! You will pay!'

Firilla was crouched in a corner, thinking of nothing but protecting her face and the front of her body, her back running with blood, when suddenly a shadow crossed the beam of light that was coming from the doorway. The girl turned,

118

startled, towards it. Firilla looked up through streaming eyes to see the figure of Glidd towering above the girl. His fist shot forward and with one blow he knocked her to the floor, then stepped over her and took Firilla in his arms.

She could hear confused sounds of shouting and running from the corridor behind him. 'Hurry,' she sobbed, 'we must get out of here! This is not a holy place!'

Still kissing her, he lifted her and ran. The corridors, which had seemed so light and so beautiful when she passed through them before, were now full of the shadows of hurrying, agitated figures.

No one but Nea had had any warning that anything was seriously wrong. When the High Priestess had not returned from her unprecedented visit to the Temple of the White Star, Nea, the only one who had known of it, had secretly climbed the forbidden stairs of the sapphire throne and looked out across the city to the temple of white crystal. What she saw there shocked her so much that she could think of nothing but revenge against the woman who, Nea was convinced, had brought this upon them. She went straight to the cell, telling no one. It was not until a man had broken through the guards at the gate, stormed through the Hall of Petitions, and gone rampaging in the forbidden inner chambers of their temple, flashing a knife and threatening to kill if he was not instantly led to his wife, that the other women became aware that their ancient stability was being destroyed. In the consequent confusion Glidd and Firilla managed to escape.

At first Glidd had no idea where to go. There was no sign of Bardek and Vallida, and the destruction of the White Temple had put the city in an uproar. Everyone seemed to be out in the streets, rushing about asking questions. No one had any answers, but the blame for the horrifying event was being put squarely on the shoulders of the Children of the Dark Star, and voices were raised everywhere against them.

As Glidd and Firilla pushed their way through the crowds, they caught a glimpse of Negg and Millon at the centre of an angry disturbance. Glidd rushed forward just in time to prevent a fight by seizing Negg's arm and pulling him out of the angry circle before he punched someone in the face. Millon pushed at him from behind but still Negg shouted insults over his shoulder and struggled to get back into the fray. They were lucky not to be pursued. Perhaps if the two marsh dwellers had not still been clad in bowman red, however dusty and torn it was, they might not have been so lucky.

'What happened?' Glidd asked Millon when they were clear.

Millon shrugged. 'You'd have thought he would be used to insults by now,' he said indifferently. 'They were saying some things about marsh dwellers . . .'

'He said . . .' Negg started up again, his face scarlet with rage.

'Never mind what he said,' interrupted Glidd hastily. 'We're all in trouble now and the last thing we want to do is attract attention to ourselves.'

Negg knew he was right. He pulled roughly away from Glidd's restraining hand and strode sulkily ahead of them, silent at last.

Firilla almost had to run to keep up with the men as they tried to put as much distance as they could between themselves and the crowd. She was covered with Glidd's short cloak to avoid being conspicuous, and kept her face half hidden behind her hair so that Nea's ugly scratches could not be seen. She kept pleading to be told where Bardek was, but at first no one would, or could, tell her.

It was Negg who turned at last and said: 'I know he got away from the Temple all right . . . I saw him and Vallida running . . .'

'I'm sure they'll be trying to return to the mountains,' added Millon, reassuringly.

'Neither they nor we will get away across the plains,' said Negg bitterly. 'All the guardians are out, fully armed, searching for us. They won't rest until they've drawn blood.'

Firilla was terrified. She had been brought up in awe of the guardians.

'It's very likely they'll let us pass,' Glidd said. 'They'll not be looking for bowmen and farmer's daughters, but for the Dark Star people.'

'But Bardek . . .'

'Bardek is a bowman.'

Just then a group of guardians came marching down the street. They were men born under the Red Star, trained to police the city. They wore leather dyed a darker shade than the bowman's red and carried a kind of crossbow far deadlier than the ordinary hunter's weapon. They were stopping people at random and questioning them. Their questioning was frequently accompanied by blows.

'Don't run,' whispered Glidd. 'But try to ease your way into that side street.'

Once this was achieved Glidd pulled them into a doorway out of sight, Firilla resting against him with her head on his shoulder, so weary and sad she did not now know how she was going to take another step. 'I have friends in Bargeda,' said Glidd. 'We can go to them. But even though they are friends I would rather they did not know our part in the destruction of the Temple, or that you are marsh dwellers.'

'Understood,' Millon said, and Negg nodded.

A safe distance from the Temple, Bardek and Vallida stopped running. The shaking of the ground had subsided and the dust had settled. Bardek was surprised to find that they were unharmed apart from minor cuts and bruises. He unstrapped the cloak he had brought for her from his back and fastened it at her throat. There was dust on her soft, pale skin and in her silver hair. He held her close and brushed it off, blowing it softly from her long lashes.

He was astonished how calm she looked. Her beautiful grey-green eyes with the golden flecks showed no trace of shock or fear. She was looking around with curiosity and pleasure.

'Come,' he said gently. 'We should not rest too long. They

could still find you and take you back.'

Something in her expression as she turned to follow him disturbed him. She seemed too calm, too obedient, too lacking in emotion. He thought of the skull which had fallen, but which he had not seen smashed. He wondered if he should return and make sure it was destroyed. Everything he had been through would have been for nothing if she was still the vehicle of the Voices. People had been killed, a whole orderly system of belief and ritual had been knocked off-balance, a proud and beautiful building had been reduced to ugly rubble. He remembered the jagged edges of crystal sticking up through the white dust like broken bones through skin, and the scream of the High Priestess as she had been crushed.

He had not thought to destroy the Whole by removing one small part, but it was effectively what he had done. 'But the system was evil,' he told himself. Vallida had said her Voices were not the 'gods' and he believed her. But the Voices and the skull, whether gods or not, had power over her. Should he go back? Should he?

He looked down at her. It was hard to believe, seeing her now so delicately beautiful, so apparently peaceful, that she had been – was – the dread Oracle.

She turned her face to his and smiled. His fears were dispelled and he took her in his arms, tilting her head back with the pressure of his lips to kiss her long and deeply. The rough cloak slipped off her shoulders, her silk flowed over his skin. Willingly at first she responded to his touch, trustingly, wonderingly . . . and then suddenly she pulled away from him, her eyes full of fear, fear of being taken over again, fear of being taken over by him.

He decided it would be too dangerous for them to pass through the town, and so he led the girl towards the east at first, planning to skirt Bar-geda and return to the shelter of the Kariva mountains when he could. The land on this side of the city was not as arid as that on the west. There was a thick ground cover of low fleshy leaves, pleasant to walk upon. Small creatures scuttled away from them and hid under rocks and bushes. They would not starve.

Vallida walked calmly beside him, but he knew that something had changed between them. She was wary of him, and if he touched he could feel her body grow tense. He reminded himself that she had seen very little of the world outside the temple and had had no experience of loving anyone before he had come so disruptively into her life. He had learned from the love of Glidd and Firilla for each other, and from his own love for them. He should have waited. He took care not to frighten her again and began to teach her about the rocks and the plants and the flowers they found growing so profusely in this part of the country. They found a marvellous variety of fungi growing on the damp underside of an overhang of rock. He told her which were good to eat and which were not. She listened to him quietly, apparently paying attention. But then, suddenly, she broke off one of the long purple filaments of one he had just told her was deadly poisonous, and before he could stop her put it in her mouth and swallowed it.

Horrified he grabbed her face and forced her mouth open, but there was no sign of it. 'Why did you do that? I told you it was poisonous! It will kill you!' he shouted angrily. He seized her shoulders roughly and shook her. All for nothing! She would die now and everything he had done would have been wasted.

Her expression was strange. He could not tell what she was thinking. Did she understand what death meant? And then he noticed that she was smiling and the smile was very cold and triumphant. Colour was draining from her cheeks, but she was smiling . . .

Suddenly he realised that the Voices had not left her, it was they who had made her eat the deadly filament. They could not bear that she should live on, independent of them.

'No!' he shouted. She was already slipping from his grasp. Her eyes were closing and she was sagging towards the ground. 'No, damn you!' If only he had destroyed the skull!

He forced her mouth open again and thrust his fingers down her throat. Firilla had once done it to him when he was very young . . .

Vallida gagged.

Furiously he persisted.

She choked and then convulsed, throwing up the dangerous fungus, still whole. She had not even bitten it in half before she swallowed it and, mercifully, the process of digestion had not begun. When she had finished she was still very pale and weak, but she seemed more herself. Her eyes when he looked into them were grateful, though she said nothing.

He carried her away from the fungi bed and found a comfortable and sheltered place. He arranged her cloak carefully on the ground and laid her on it, pillowing her head on a little pile of soft twigs and leaves.

'Sleep,' he said gently. 'We'll not go on until we've rested.'

She turned her face from him with such a movement of weariness and despair that his heart ached. He bent down and brushed away some strands of soft hair from her cheek. Her lids closed heavily as though she were already asleep, but as he watched he saw that tears were seeping from under her lashes.

He sat beside her on a rock for a long time, watching her closely until her breathing became gentle and regular, his mind drifting over all that had happened and wondering about all that was to come. He feared that the skull was probably buried deep in the hill where he would never be able to find it. She would never be free. How long would it take the priesthood to rebuild the temple . . . and would its power ever be the same . . .

He leant towards Vallida and stroked her hair. Her expression now was peaceful and relaxed, as though she were an ordinary person enjoying a restful sleep in a comfortable bed. At least he had given her that!

Slowly, as he grew drowsier and drowsier, it seemed as

though his mind were floating free, as it had done that time in the marshes. He seemed to be leaving the planet, seemed to be travelling beyond it into the far reaches of the sky until he could see the great Stars that had ruled their lives since before memory, and they no longer looked so great or so powerful . . .

Was Agaron no more than dust floating in an infinite universe?

At this moment Vallida turned in her sleep and her hand fell against his knee. The feeling of strangeness, of being out in space beyond their world, ceased. His vision contracted to her silver hair, her soft flesh, and the shining silk that flowed about her body.

In Bar-geda Glidd found the friends he was looking for, Jain and Na, a couple he often stayed with when he came to the city for provisions. The tired little group were made welcome and given shelter. Firilla's scratches were attended to and she was put to bed, exhausted. To explain the scratches and the weary dusty state they were in Glidd told his friends that they had just arrived in the city from the mountains, and their journey over the plains had been a difficult one, Firilla having been attacked by a wild purr-cat.

They pretended to know nothing of the recent events at the White Temple, and were told in great detail how a party of marsh dwellers, joining with the robbers and vagabonds who lived hidden in the city, had attacked the Temple and overthrown it.

'This is bad news,' Glidd said. 'How many were they?'

'A hundred at least, probably more.'

'What is happening now? Are these hundred still loose?'

'Some of them. But the guardians set fire to the tunnel where they come from and destroyed their filthy holes. Those who had managed to get back to hiding have been smoked out and killed. Those who are still free will not be so for long.'

A dark and bitter look passed between Negg and Millon. Glidd felt sick. His city friends noticed nothing wrong and chattered on.

Na, slicing up the leaf-food for the meal, said: 'They say the guardians are going to raid the marshes and clear them out once and for all. It is a terrible thing that parents let these creatures live. No one is safe while the least one of them is left alive.'

'But are they sure it was the people of the Dark Star?'

'Who else?' Jain asked.

Glidd was silent, thinking. To prevent further bloodshed it was clear that they must give themselves up . . . but if they did Firilla would be punished with them, and that he couldn't bear. He thought back to when she had pleaded with him to let her son live. They had both known then that they were committing a great folly, probably a dangerous one, but how dangerous they could not have guessed.

Na served the meal and they ate, but not one of the three tasted the food. Each was separately deep in thought.

Meanwhile Firilla dreamed that she had joined a great host of spirit-beings, swooping and circling in flight far from the planet Agaron, beyond the Seven Stars, beyond the furthest reaches of the universe. She was conscious of herself thinking, but could not see or feel any kind of body. She and the beings seemed to flow through darkness like wisps of light, keeping together, moving purposefully, though she was not aware of what the purpose was. Nebulae began to appear out of the darkness, stars and planets, appearing and disappearing as though they were lights pulsing on and off, on and off, each beat of the pulse countless aeons apart.

Suddenly, the group of beings she was with began to swoop down upon a planet like feathered whains upon a field of grain. She plunged when they plunged and found herself choking on air as a drowning swimmer on water. The lightness she had experienced as a spirit had gone and she was trapped in a cage of bone, weighted down with flesh . . .

She longed to be free again, and at last she got her wish

for she found herself rising . . .

'We're travellers,' she cried as she woke. 'We're passing by. This planet is not our home!' She sat up and looked into the troubled eyes of Glidd. 'There are places we go to, and places we come from!'

'And there are places that we're responsible for,' Glidd added sadly. He had made his decision. He did not know what Firilla had dreamed, or why she cried out what she did, but he did know that even travellers have responsibilities to the places they pass through.

He took her in his arms and told her how many innocent people were being punished for what they had helped to do, and that he had decided to go before the Council of Governors and confess that it was he, a bowman, who had committed the sacrilege. Firilla clung to him, forgetting the joyful message of her dream.

'If the Governors are just they will listen to my reasons,' he said soothingly. 'And though I can't expect to escape punishment, they'll at least know that something is very wrong and hopefully will set it right.'

'I am to blame for all this,' Firilla wept. 'If I hadn't kept my son alive none of this would have happened. I'll go before them . . .'

'No.'

'I'll not let you go alone.'

'You must go back to the mountains. Bardek will need you.'

She hesitated. She longed to see Bardek, but she knew that he no longer needed her. 'My place is with you and I'll not leave you!' And Glidd knew by the way she said it that she meant it, and that they would not be parted no matter what befell them. He held her close and neither spoke for a long while. Then she asked for Negg and Millon and was told they had returned to the marshes while she slept. She was shocked.

'They're in danger!' she cried, her voice as caring as if they were her own family.

127

Glidd kissed the top of her head and smiled.

'So you love marsh dwellers now?' he said gently, and then, more gravely: 'Whether we like it or not my love, we have questioned the Laws of Agaron and we cannot go back to our old ways of thinking.'

She sighed. 'If only I knew what had happened to Bardek I'd be able to face whatever we have to face more easily.'

His arms tightened around her, his chin resting on her hair. Whatever she knew, or did not know, it would not be easy to face what they had to face.

CHAPTER 11

The Blue Smoke and the Choosing

The Council of Governors had been in almost continuous session since the destruction of the White Temple. The retaliation of the guardians against the people of the Dark Star had caused those who had escaped to join in bitterness with others of their kind to attack whatever they could of the orderly society that had excluded them and now unjustly punished them for something they had not done.

Acts of violence became commonplace, acts of repression more cruel to meet them. Reports of disaffection and the disintegration of order were pouring in to the archivists at the Palace of the Governors. It was almost impossible to get them all recorded on the memory-coils, or processed in the punishment offices.

But despite all this, in the two stricken temples, the priests and priestesses strove to continue as much as they could of the ancient rituals.

In the Temple of the Blue Star a new High Priestess had to be found, and the Ceremony of the Choosing was started.

Nea, when she had recovered from Glidd's blow, went straight to Maya's chambers and locked herself in, to emerge only when she knew that the Choosing was taking place in the high domed hall of the sapphire throne.

As novice she was not eligible to be chosen, nor to have any part in the ceremony, but Maya had been so much in love with her she had given in to her demand for certain gifts that it would have been better she had refused. Amongst these was a collar representing a great winged Harpy, a creature with the face and the body of a woman, but the wings and claws of a garrar. It was worked in gold with sapphire eyes and crown of mirror-stone, and was part of her essential equipment as High Priestess.

Nea wore it now over Maya's ribbon dress and stepped confidently into the Hall of the Choosing. The junior priestesses at the entrance came forward to hold her back, but the sacred collar around her shoulders and on her breast made them hesitate. She passed them by and strode into the Hall.

In the centre, at the foot of the steep stairway that led to the sapphire throne, there was a brazier of blue fire around which the senior priestesses eligible for the Ceremony were gathered. Ritual words were passing from one to the other in low and monotonous tones, while the strong and potent scent of the blue flames had its effect. Gradually their eyes were glazing. Nea knew that once one of them had entered trance she would have lost her opportunity. Everything depended on her making use of the effect of the smoke before any of the others did, and mounting the stair ahead of them.

She broke into the circle and leant her face close to the flames. At first the searing heat drove her back, but she leant again, her eyes shut, breathing in the hot hallucinogenic fumes of the mezmer plant. Her eyebrows and her eyelashes were singed, her skin began to blister, but still she breathed the precious smoke, for it was customary for the first priestess to fall into trance to climb the stairs and claim the crown of mirror-stone.

The others were so bemused by the chanting and the scent they were only partly aware of her intrusion. Those who were not part of the Choosing saw what was happening but were too afraid to interfere. It was believed that if a woman were interrupted while breathing the blue flame she would be claimed by the Dark Lord. Besides, Nea had the collar of the High Priestess, and no one wearing it had ever been questioned or touched.

Suddenly Nea screamed. Her hair was a sheet of blue flame. She leapt forward, beating frantically at her head, knocking over the brazier which strewed its brilliant jewels of fire over the marble floor, scattering the onlookers. She reached the bottom step of the stairs, but even as she reached it another of the priestesses who had entered trance leapt forward too.

This was unprecedented. The non-contenders screamed and clung together with horror. Those who had failed fell to the floor moaning, locked in private dreams of ecstasy, forgetting their attempt to mount the way to absolute power.

Nea staggered with the pain of the fire in her hair, and in the time it took her to beat the flames out, the other priestess, Kirini, had passed her and was already climbing to the throne. But Nea had not suffered what she had suffered to make way for someone else. She scrambled after her.

As though it were not enough that the Temple of the White Star had crumbled like a sand castle, the ancient ritual of the Choosing of the High Priestess of the Blue Star was being desecrated by ambition and violence. But although Nea had cheated, there was no doubt she was in trance. She totally believed she was the woman-breasted, feather-winged Harpy whose image she wore about her neck. Her screams as she leapt up the steep steps after Kirini were to her the blood-curdling cries of the Harpy on the hunt, closing on its prey. She did not use her hands to pull the priestess back, but lunged at her with her claws.

Twice she made contact, twice she drew blood. Kirini staggered but continued on her way. Her trance image of herself was that she was rising on a spiral of blue mist, each turn of the spiral carrying her nearer and nearer to the Source of Blue Light in the brilliant depths of the Star. The pain she felt as Nea tore at her she believed to be no more than the twinges of memory from her old nature, which she knew she must now leave behind if she were to enter the inner sanctum of the goddess of the Blue Star.

Seeing that the woman ahead was widening the gap between them, the Harpy lifted its wings and swooped upon her. Kirini, turning her private spiral, only partially aware of the danger, swayed instinctively aside.

The watchers down below in the hall gasped to see Nea fling herself into the air in the direction of the priestess, miss her, and hurtle over the edge of the stairs, to fall with a dreadful thud to the marble floor.

Some rushed forward to see if she were still alive, others craned upwards to see if the victorious priestess had reached the throne. All were in confusion.

There had never been a Choosing like this, and everyone was terrified as to what it might mean. Was everything they had ever known and trusted to be destroyed? How would they live their lives if the ancient patterns were no more? They knew that the whole was dependent on the parts and the parts dependent on the whole. To destroy one was to threaten all.

Those who were looking up saw Kirini reach the throne at last, take the crown of mirror-stone and place it on her head. They gave a sigh. Once again they had a High Priestess who would tell them what to do. In silence they waited for her first command.

Bardek and Vallida, making their way through the low eastern hills, came upon a small broken down cabin, a nomad shepherd's hut, long disused, the roof almost weathered away. They took shelter and rested a while, pretending that they were 'togethered', and this was their home. There was no food, but a few rusted utensils. Blankets made of fear-all fur had worn into holes. In a corner they found some dusty parchments and drew them out in surprise. It was an unusual shepherd who could read. But when they looked more closely they saw that the words were in the archaic language and the drawings were enigmatic. It was more than likely that the nomad had found them somewhere on his wanderings in search of fresh pastures and kept them, thinking that perhaps he could trade them for something more useful one day.

Bardek went hunting for their meal and was gone longer than he intended. When he returned he found Vallida still poring over the parchments. 'Do you understand them?' he asked with surprise, realising how little he knew about her.

'This part here is a star map,' she said confidently.

Bardek craned over her shoulder and she started to point out features to him. Agaron itself seemed to be a planet circled by five moons, and itself circling a star which was by no means the greatest amongst those shown. He remembered the strange vision he had had in which Agaron and its 'stars' had seemed so small and insignificant in the universe.

'Whoever made this,' he said excitedly, 'could not have been part of our civilisation. It is blasphemy for us to think that there is anything greater than our Seven Stars.'

And then he frowned. Why seven? Five moons and one sun made six. Five moons and one sun made one star! He began to understand with what efficiency the people of Agaron were governed when the authority of the Temples was never questioned. Then another thought struck him that made his heart skip a beat. If the Seven Stars were not the most powerful forces in the universe, if their significance had been given them by man, then the curse he bore as a Child of the Dark Star had no meaning. He was neither cursed, nor blessed. He was free.

But even as this thought took hold, he was startled by a sudden change in Vallida. She seized the knife from his belt and started to stab at the parchment, her face distorted with fury.

'Vallida!' he shouted, and tried to take the knife from her, but she pulled it away from him with a sudden extraordinary strength. She flung the ripped parchment on to the floor and then faced him, holding the knife like a professional hunter or guardian, ready to strike at him. He made another grab at the hand with the knife but she moved too fast, and came back at him so swiftly that had he not leapt aside he would have been seriously hurt.

He didn't know what to do. He knew it was not Vallida wielding the knife. With all his heart he wanted to destroy whoever it was that was using her body, but would he not destroy the girl as well?

'Why do you want us to see no further than Agaron!' he shouted to the unknown using her body, dodging the lunging knife. 'Why are you so afraid of questioning?' Was it possible the Dark Lord himself ruled the planet and that all the priests and all the temples were but dupes of his?

It suddenly crossed Bardek's mind that he must kill Vallida if he wanted to destroy the Oracle and the sinister Voices that were still using her. Was it possible that they clung so tenaciously to her because she was the only vehicle they could use? If this was so, his duty, if he wanted to free Agaron from a rule he was increasingly learning to distrust, was to destroy her.

With fierce determination he seized her wrist and twisted it. The knife was at her throat before he remembered that the Voices themselves had tried to kill her with the poisonous fungi. It was they who wanted her dead and, having failed before, they were now using him to try to kill her. They were using him! With horror he realised the implications of this.

Suddenly Vallida's voice laughed – a cold, hard, mocking laugh – and he stared at her, knowing that they had read his mind.

'Read this,' he thought fiercely. 'I'm getting your measure and when I have it completely you will be finished. As each moment passes I learn more about you. One thing I've just learned is that you fear independent thought. Your power only works when people resign themselves to you. Well,' he glared at the eyes of the girl behind which the dread Being raged, 'I do not resign. I will not resign.'

Suddenly Vallida's expression changed. She gave a sigh and fell to the ground. He was beside her in an instant, lifting her in his arms, kissing her, overwhelmed with the relief of having her back. She looked at him with hurt and bewildered eyes. 'Never mind,' he whispered, 'you've been away, but you have returned.'

'Bardek,' she said in a voice so faint he had to lean his ear to her mouth to catch it. 'Hold me.'

He was already holding her, but he held her closer.

CHAPTER 12

The Sleepers

In Bar-geda, Glidd and Firilla were 'Before the Governors'. This meant they were put into a small room and told to speak into a little gadget on a stand. They were then left and the door tightly locked.

Somewhere in another part of the building the twelve Governors, who had been given office when they were named by the Oracle, sat at a round table with the symbol of their power in the centre. Ironically it was a sword embedded in a stone, a symbol brought from Earth, its meaning long since lost.

When they were in session they saw no one face to face, for in direct contact with a person communication can be on many different levels, a hundred tiny movements and nuances of sound can give clues to things that are not said, thoughts can transfer, invisible energies can transmit . . . A judge face to face with a criminal picks up subtleties of feeling and makes his final decision often by intuition as much as by Law. On Agaron this was avoided as much as possible. The Governors in their role of judges were deliberately isolated, all sound and sight of the accused filtered through impersonal microphones and cameras, devices themselves unknown to the common man and therefore frightening. What they saw and heard and what they judged was the very barest of bare 'truths', so bare indeed that their understanding bore very little relation to true understanding, and therefore very little relation to justice.

Firilla and Glidd sat on the chairs provided in their cell,

close together, hand in hand, too nervous even to talk to each other.

Glidd was told by a disembodied voice to speak, and the instruction had to be repeated several times before he finally cleared his throat and began. He told their story as simply and directly as he could, with only two partial untruths in it. He suggested that Bardek and the Oracle had been killed during the collapse of the Temple, and he made no mention of Negg and Millon.

Firilla listened to him and her heart sank; if only they could see their judges she was sure Glidd would be able to speak with greater sincerity and conviction, but how could one speak to a gadget and expect it to respond to the levels of meaning behind the words, to feel for the reasons they had done what they had.

After he had finished speaking they sat in silence for a long time, regretting what he had said, wishing he had another chance to put it in better words.

Suddenly there was a crackle in the air and they looked up, clutching hands more tightly than before.

'You will be stripped of all the privileges of your Star signs,' a voice said. 'You will have the mark of the Dark Star entered against you. You will then be executed.'

Glidd took Firilla in his arms, numb with shock. They knew that no one but the people of the Dark Star were ever executed and had not dreamed that this fate could be theirs. Glidd looked angrily at the place from which the voice had issued.

'Is this all?' he shouted furiously. 'Are you not going to investigate the injustices we told you about, and set right the things that are wrong?'

The light went out in their cell and they were in the pitch dark. Firilla remembered the cell she had been in before and began to sob.

'It was you who broke the Star Law of Agaron,' the disembodied voice boomed out again, and it seemed to come from all around them, reverberating in their very flesh. 'You cannot now claim its protection.'

And then there was silence.

Suddenly the floor gave way beneath them and they dropped sickeningly to hurtle down a kind of chute. Screaming, Firilla found herself separated from Glidd. She could hear his voice calling her as she was bashed from side to side on the downward rush – but she could not reach him.

Negg and Millon hurried back to the marshlands to warn the tribes there of the growing violence against the people of the Dark Star, and the threat of attack hanging over the marshes. They were alarmed to see how low the Red Star had sunk. The time of the Dark Star was approaching and even marsh dwellers did not care to be abroad in such cold and dark.

They increased their pace, although they were already exhausted, until at last they could see the long low stain of the reed beds and the occasional glint of water. The colour of the sky was deepening with the Star's sinking. The light was dimming.

'What are we doing?' Millon suddenly asked, stopping short. 'We have no tribe. We owe these people nothing!'

Negg stopped a few paces ahead of him and looked back. What he had said was true, but . . . he could not define his feelings, his need to do what he was doing. Before meeting Bardek he had had no purpose but day to day survival; no loyalty but to himself and to his tribe . . . which was, after all, only an extension of himself. Now he had an indefinable yearning to be part of . . . to extend beyond himself . . . to see further . . . to understand more. Life as he had known it was not enough.

'I can't explain,' he said almost apologetically to Millon. 'But knowing what I now know, I have to warn them.'

'They'll not thank you. As likely as not you'll get a spear down your throat before you can say a word.'

'I have to try. Don't you see . . . we can't leave things as they are. We – they – have never had a chance. Now we have. Things are changing.'

Millon sighed wearily. 'We'll accomplish nothing.'

'We might accomplish something,' Negg said. 'Besides,' he added with a wry look, 'we've come so far, what else can we do?'

He started off towards the marshes again, and, after a while, Millon followed him.

So swiftly did Firilla slide down the chute and so icily did the dark air rush past her that she felt as though she were suspended in Time, the difference between an aeon and a moment imperceptible. She hit the ground with tremendous force, darkness instantly extinguishing her thoughts.

When she regained consciousness she cried out at once for Glidd. Her head and her limbs ached. The deep scratches Nea had given her had opened again and she could feel sticky blood trickling down her cheek, but she could move, and by some miracle was not seriously damaged. Her eyes gradually grew used to the darkness and she began to distinguish faint shapes around her. There was a mysterious and very faint glow that seemed to come uniformly from every direction. In its dim light she saw that she was in a strange and cavernous place, surrounded by twisting roots and dark columns, at the centre of a sinister web of shadow. Terrified, she called again for Glidd and heard a groan from the ground to the left of the chute. Glidd was lying there rubbing his head and painfully trying to rise. Sobbing, she ran to him and gathered him in her arms.

'I was so afraid without you,' she said. 'Where are we? What is this place?'

He was still too dazed to speak, but she chattered on, overwhelmed with relief that he was still alive, the sound of her own voice a comfort.

'Do you think we're supposed to be dead now? Was that the execution?'

He shook his head feebly.

'Can we escape? Surely we can escape! This is a huge

place, surely we can hide! They'll never find us here.'

Glidd recovered enough to look carefully around. The furthest reaches were in darkness and it was not possible to see where the cavern ended or if, indeed, it ended at all. They seemed alone, but any number of creatures could be hiding behind the stone columns that held up the ceiling and the roots of the trenoids that hung from above, continuously, eerily, but infinitesimally moving in search of solid ground. It was an uncanny place, cold and damp and dreadfully quiet. His first hope that because there was light there must be an opening faded as he realised that the glow was coming from the rocks themselves. He had heard of such rocks, but had never seen them before.

He raised himself cautiously, wincing, to a standing position by pushing on Firilla's shoulders. His ankle was rapidly swelling, but luckily it was a sprain and not a break.

'I think we should at least make it difficult for them to find us,' he said.

Leaning on her, he guided her away from the chute. They made their way further into the cavern, looking nervously round as they walked, expecting at any moment to find their executioner.

It was impossible to tell how long they struggled through the cavern. There was no Star to give them time or direction. No rising and no setting. The dim faint light that was diffused throughout was constant and impassive. It told them nothing.

At last they had to rest. From where they sat close together the cavern stretched in every direction, every feature repeated a hundred times so that there was no way of knowing whether they had been travelling in a circle or not. 'This cavern must be under the whole of the city,' mused Glidd, and wished he could tell under which part of it they were. He peered up at the ceiling and wondered if it were possible to excavate their way through to the outer world. The ceiling was very high, but it might just be possible if he climbed some of the larger roots . . . But what could he use as a tool?

His knife had been taken from him before his confession. The buckle on his belt, almost the size of his hand, was the hardest thing he had on him. He looked at it thoughtfully, feeling the sharpness of its edge. Firilla had a smaller one, but it too was made of metal and would serve.

He looked again at the weighty darkness above them and his courage nearly failed. To hold a city the size of Bar-geda the ground must be thick and hard indeed. They could dig at it with their puny tools until the stars grew cold and not reach a quarter through. Dispiritedly he sat down with his back against a column and shut his eyes. He could feel Firilla kneeling beside him and winced as she touched his ankle to bind it with a strip of cloth torn from her skirt. How were they to get out of this gloomy place? How?

Having finished the binding, Firilla sat down close against him and rested her head upon his shoulder. 'Perhaps the execution is by slow starvation,' she whispered, hoping he would deny it.

'Perhaps,' he murmured, the pain in his ankle throbbing with the regularity of a drum beat. 'Perhaps.' But in his heart he knew that was exactly what it was. Babies born under the Dark Star were exposed in the desert and were said to die of 'natural causes'. Their own horoscopes would be tampered with in the Hall of Records and they, bowman and farmer, would become 'children of the Dark Star', they too dying of natural causes. An ironic fate considering their decision at Bardek's birth.

He held Firilla close and wondered how it would be at the end. Who would die first? Would they lose their minds and prey on each other for survival? He shuddered, fearing the last moments almost more than death itself.

'I think . . .' Firilla said softly, and then stopped.

He was so lost in his own dark thoughts he didn't hear her, nor did he notice that her whole body was now tensed for listening. 'I think,' she whispered again, lifting her mouth to his ear so that her words scarcely travelled through the air, 'we are not alone.' This time he paid attention.

He looked at her sharply and followed her eyes as she glanced to the side. He fancied he saw a slight movement.

Firilla gripped his arm tightly and he could feel her trembling. What creature lurked in these dim regions? It struck him that they might not die of starvation after all, but as sustenance for another.

The shadow they had glimpsed moved again and the instinct of the hunter was roused. Glidd had no bow, no knife, but he had the sudden realisation that whoever or whatever was hunting him could in turn be hunted. If he could be food for it, it was more than probable it could be food for him.

He pushed Firilla aside and tensed his muscles, every faculty alert.

The shadow darted from one column to another.

Glidd sprang towards it, but the sudden movement drove a dagger of pain through his ankle and he fell to the ground. Cursing, he dragged himself up, but the shadow was out of reach behind a further column.

He may have failed to seize it, but at least it was on the defensive now. He started in pursuit, painfully slow on his damaged foot, Firilla close behind. Each time they were near enough to contemplate attack the shadow retreated.

They were encouraged. The creature was afraid of them.

Deeper and deeper into the cavern they penetrated, the shadow always just ahead of them. Occasionally they came upon bones. Human bones. Firilla shuddered and made sure to keep close to Glidd, who began to wonder if they were being led to a lair where others of its kind were waiting to pounce on them.

At times it seemed to be moving on two legs, upright, like themselves, and Glidd was convinced it was a man. But even as he thought this something in its movement suggested an animal.

'I think it's leading us somewhere,' Firilla whispered nervously. 'Could it be friendly?'

'If it were friendly why doesn't it stop and let us catch up?'

'But we are pursuing it. It thinks that we are predators.'

Glidd stopped. She was right. They stood still for a long time watching the column behind which the creature had disappeared. Glidd did not relax for an instant.

Suddenly Firilla broke from his side and, before he realised what she was about to do, walked boldly out into an open area between columns. 'Friend,' she called out in a sweet and friendly voice, holding out her hands to show they were empty. 'Come to us. Don't be afraid.' And because there was genuinely no thought of harming it in her mind, her voice rang true.

Glidd broke out in a sweat, half wanting to haul her back, half glad she had done it. He was ready to spring, and this time he was determined to keep upright no matter how painful the foot was.

Nothing happened for a while, and Firilla herself was contemplating retreat, when suddenly the thing appeared from behind the column and stood in the open not far from her.

It was human: a wizened child, his limbs twisted and deformed. Firilla's mother's heart went out to him at once and she took a step towards him. Glidd cried out warningly and his voice rang through the cavern, the reverberations of it shaking dust from the ceiling. The boy almost fled at the sound, but the longing he had for other human company was so strong, and the woman before him looked so kind and beautiful, that he waited.

Glidd allowed her to go right up to the child, realising that if he interfered they might lose him. Like a mountain fear-all the boy stood, ready to run, watching her with alert and curious eyes.

'Don't be afraid,' she said gently. 'We'll not harm you. What is your name?'

The child said nothing, but put his head on one side and looked her over carefully.

'My name is Firilla,' she said soothingly. 'I am of the Green Star. This is Glidd, a bowman of the Red.'

The tattered rags that covered the boy's limbs gave very little indication of his birth star, but she thought they might have been yellow once. She wondered what crime a child such as this could have committed to be punished in this way.

'Firilla,' she repeated, pointing. 'And Glidd.'

Glidd nodded and smiled, seeing now they had nothing to fear from the urchin.

'Servant,' the boy suddenly said, putting his hand on his own chest.

'But what is you name?' Firilla said gently.

The boy looked puzzled. 'Servant is my name,' he said.

Glidd and she looked at one another. Perhaps he had been in these dark regions so long he had forgotten his name. The deformation of his limbs indicated that he had been without proper nourishment for a long, long time.

But he was still alive and this gave them hope.

What food did he have? However inadequate it appeared to be, it was keeping him alive.

'If you are a servant,' Glidd said, limping forward to confront the boy, 'whom do you serve?'

'The Sleepers,' the boy said at once.

'The Sleepers?'

'Come, I show you.' He loped off without waiting to see if they followed. Now that they had seen him properly, the oddities of movement they had noted in the shadow became explicable. He could move quite fast with his strange, ungainly gait, and was already quite a distance from them.

'Don't let's lose him,' Firilla cried and hurried forward. Glidd, hobbling after her, cursed the pain in his foot.

The boy paused from time to time, rather impatiently, waiting for them to catch up, but at last he stopped. He stooped, turned something they could not see on the floor with his hands. It seemed to be stiff, for he put a great deal of effort into it, but eventually there was a creaking sound and light suddenly flooded into the cavern from below the boy's feet, illuminating his face so grotesquely they both pulled up sharply, wondering if they had been right to follow him.

But light! Whatever menace they might have to face at least light would make it more endurable.

Glidd put himself in front of Firilla and moved forward cautiously. The boy began to disappear into the light, feet first. Glidd ignored his sprained ankle and limped forward quickly to get a closer look at what was happening. The boy was climbing down into a hole filled with light.

Firilla dashed forward. 'Don't go,' she cried. 'Don't leave us.'

'You come too,' said the boy. 'I show you the Sleepers.'

He beckoned to them. Glidd peered down, but because of the contrast between the semi-darkness they were in and the brilliance of the light below, he was temporarily blinded. If they climbed down into it they would be at the mercy of whoever or whatever was below.

'We must trust him,' whispered Firilla. 'There's nothing else for us to do.'

Glidd nodded and followed the boy. At the foot of the ladder he found himself in another cavern, but this was cut out of the white chalk layer below the dark rock and soil of the upper cavern. Artificial light sticks were on the walls, reflecting off the chalk, making the whole place dazzling. There was no one there besides the boy. Glidd called Firilla and she climbed down to join them. The boy touched something on the wall and the lid covering the hole clanged shut. Glidd shouted at once for him to open it again, as though the cavern above, for all that it held nothing but discomfort and death for them, was a familiar place they were unwilling to be cut off from. But the boy took no notice and ran off down one of the narrow corridors that led away from the small area they were in.

Glidd and Firilla, anxious not to lose him, followed close behind. The floor seemed to be slanting. giving the impression that they were going deeper and deeper into the chalk. 'Stop!' Glidd cried at last. The boy, some way ahead, stopped and looked back enquiringly. 'Where are you taking us? This is not the way out.'

'There is no way out. I take you to the Sleepers.'

Firilla bit her lip and took Glidd's hand. 'Perhaps he means the dead,' she said nervously.

'Who are these Sleepers?' Glidd asked.

'My masters. I serve them.'

'Do you serve them by yourself, or are there other servants to help you?'

'By myself. My mother and my father used to do the work, but they are dead.' He looked sad.

Good, thought Glidd, at least he knows the difference between the sleeping and the dead.

'You poor child,' said Firilla.

'So it is just you down here and . . . the Sleepers?' Glidd asked.

'Yes.'

'Will the Sleepers not be awake now?'

'They do not wake. They sleep.'

Glidd indicated to the boy to carry on, and he and Firilla followed as before. He was intrigued.

At last they reached a chamber where the chalk had been smoothed back to make flat walls. In the centre was a long low table on which lay seven sealed caskets of transparent crystal, each a different colour, the colours corresponding to the Stars of Agaron.

The boy pointed to them. 'My masters,' he said proudly.

Glidd and Firilla moved forward and gasped at what they saw. In six of the caskets were figures, apparently fast asleep. The blue and the green were women, the rest men. At the bottom of each casket, near their feet, was a little panel of dials and lights. Glidd and Firilla passed from one body to the other along the line, marvelling at the extraordinary sight. 'How long have they been asleep?' Glidd asked curiously.

The boy shrugged and shook his head.

'As long as you can remember?'

He nodded.

'Do they ever wake?'

He shook his head.

'What do you do for them?'

He pointed to the panels and dials. 'Sometimes they dream and that light on the screen moves up and down along that line. If it moves up and down too much I have to turn this knob here, this way,' he said, touching it carefully and indicating a turn to the right.

'Do you know why?'

'My father said because their dreams were bad then and we must help them to have better dreams.'

'If you didn't turn it, what would happen?'

He looked puzzled. 'I don't know. I do what my father told me.'

Glidd moved up and down the line of Sleepers, fascinated. He noted that the casket made of dark smoky quartz was empty. He paused a moment beside it, thinking, then moved on. 'Do you feed them?'

'No.'

'How do they stay alive then?'

Servant shrugged and shook his head. It was not a question he had ever asked himself.

'How do you stay alive?'

The boy looked puzzled.

'What do you eat?'

He recognised the question and took them aside to show them a little pill dispenser on the wall.

'Pills! Firilla and I are hungry. May we have some of your pills?' The boy shook his head. 'Only pills for Servant come out.'

'Surely you can share with us?'

'Only pills for Servant.'

'If we helped you look after the Sleepers?'

The boy hesitated. 'I don't know. I can't get the pills when I want them. They come by themselves at certain times.'

Glidd felt defeated; it was a pre-set dispenser, probably unalterable, with just enough sustenance for one.

'Did your mother and father have pills?' Firilla asked suddenly. Glidd looked at her approvingly.

'Yes.'

'Show us where their pills came out.'

Servant showed them other dispensers and watched impassively while Glidd and Firilla banged and shook each one of them in turn. No pills came out.

'No more pills from those,' Servant said.

'Did they stop before your parents died,' Glidd asked, 'or afterwards.'

'Before.'

Glidd and Firilla stood before the empty dispensers, their hopes destroyed. The boy's was the last dispenser. Obviously the parents, knowing that their food supply was finished and that they would soon die, had instructed the boy to carry on their duties. It was possible that for a while they had shared his food pills with him, and that is why he was so undernourished. But then they must have decided to allow themselves to die so that he could live.

Glidd and Firilla looked along the wall at the other dispensers. There must have been many other servants, probably generations of them. Through the transparent base of the last dispenser they could see that only a few pills were left. What happened when they were gone? Would the Sleepers wake and look after themselves? And if they did, what would they eat? Or would they destroy themselves with bad dreams?

Firilla sat down on a low stool in the corner of the room. She felt weak already from lack of food, and very near to despair.

'This one,' the boy said, as if he wanted to distract them from the dispensers, pointing to the white casket, 'and this one,' to the blue, 'have had very bad dreams lately. I have never seen the line jump so much. A little while ago they both jumped at the same time and I had ever so much trouble turning the knobs fast enough to bring them to the right level. Even when I had turned them they kept going back to the danger mark.'

149

Glidd was looking very thoughtful. 'I wonder what would happen if we woke them?'

The boy was horrified. 'It is forbidden!'

'Who forbids it?'

Servant's eyes were almost starting out of his thin little face with dismay that such a thing should even be contemplated. 'It is forbidden,' he repeated in a hushed voice.

Glidd looked at the lines on the screens of the white and blue Sleepers. The white had a certain irregularity about it, but the blue was moving along as evenly as the others. The face of the man in the red casket twitched slightly, and they noticed that the line on his screen which had been moving more strongly up and down than the others began to flatten out. Servant did not look alarmed and did nothing to adjust the knob.

'I thought . . .' said Glidd.

'No, that is normal. They each do that in turn. I only do anything when the lines reach the edges of the screens and seem to be out of control, or when they look as if they are dreaming out of sequence.'

Firilla rose from the stool and came to stand next to Glidd. She leant against him, holding his hand, looking down at the regular tracing of the lines on the screen of the Red Sleeper.

A slight sound came from the wall. The boy leapt at it, and, before they realised what was going on, he had seized a small pill that slid out of the dispenser and popped it into his mouth.

He looked at them defiantly as he swallowed it. It had not escaped him that they might try to steal his pills.

CHAPTER 13

Ancient Records

Bardek and Vallida, locked in each other's arms, slept long and soundly. When Bardek eventually woke he raised himself on his elbow the better to look down on the girl curled against him. Gently he moved the strands of hair that had fallen over her face and drew his fingertips lightly over her cheek. When he stooped and touched his lips to hers she stirred and smiled, though her eyes were not yet open.

'We should move on and find some proper shelter,' he said softly. 'I have no fire powders and the time of the Dark Star is very cold. We should not have slept so long.' He wondered if she had ever experienced the dark and the cold locked away in her white and shining temple.

She opened her eyes and looked round curiously. He helped her to sit up and she leant against his chest. He kissed the nape of her neck, and her hair, his arms tightening around her, wanting to make love to her. She shivered as a cold wind started up and rustled the leaves and the hollow stick-plants near them. He caught an expression in her eyes as she looked over his shoulder that made him forget his feelings and turn quickly to see what she had seen. Something or someone strange and dark was moving on the top of a low knoll. Bardek felt instinctively for the knife in his belt, freeing himself from the clinging soft silk of her dress and the sweet sensation of her body.

The man, for man Bardek was now convinced it was, was in shadow. A long dark cloak flowed from his shoulders to the ground and on his head was what appeared to be a tall crown of dark feathers.

Bardek was startled and suddenly recalled Glidd's persistent concern over the crown of garrar feathers he had had in the mountains. He stood up, clutching his knife.

'Who are you?' he demanded, though he feared he knew the answer.

The figure remained silent. The only sound was the sound the wind made . . .

'I've seen him before,' Vallida whispered.

'Who is he?' breathed Bardek.

She shook her head.

The fading light was playing tricks and the man who had seemed so solid seemed now to be dissolving in front of them.

Bardek plunged forward, but when he reached the knoll a shadow seemed to float away. All he found was the crown of black feathers resting on a stone as though it had been placed deliberately for him to find, and the cloak, caught in a bush, billowing in the wind.

The crown was magnificent. The ring that held it to the head was of gold studded with jet and ruby. Rising from the ring were alternate spurs of obsidian and ruby, splinters of black and red light. Between them, tufts of garrar feathers glowed red and black like the ones he had found as a child. He picked it up and turned it round and round in his hands, absorbed by the beauty of it. As a child he had felt powerful and confident wearing that makeshift crown and he could not resist the temptation now to wear this one. He lifted it to his head.

'No!' cried Vallida, running forward. 'Bardek! Put it down!'

He heard her voice as though she were a long, long distance away. He looked at her, the white silk of her dress billowing around her, her silver hair floating. But, as sometimes happens in dreams, with every step she took towards him she seemed to be getting further and further away.

'Put it down! Please put it down.' Her voice was thin like

the wind through distant reeds. The crown was rising in his hands almost without his willing it. He knew he would put it on, and he knew also that he should not, he was being used as Vallida had been used. With one part of his mind he knew this, but with another part he did not care.

He held the crown a few inches above his head, pausing before he lowered it. In that pause the part of him that was still his own was quite calm and logical. He knew that he wanted to put the crown on. He wanted to, irrespective of whoever else wanted him to.

He fitted the crown to his head and stooped for the cloak.

Vallida stopped running and stood horrified, staring at him. He was transformed. The Dark Lord himself could not have looked more fearful or more splendid.

He smiled. He held out his arms to her. He felt confident, powerful, strong.

'Vallida,' he commanded, 'come to me.'

She drew back, shaking her head. He took a step towards her, but she turned to run.

'Vallida,' he cried.

She lifted her flowing skirts and ran as swiftly as she could away from him. He realised that in the shadowy landscape with numerous rocks and bushes she would not have to go far to be completely hidden from him. He started in pursuit.

'Vallida! Vallida!' But she was like a fear-all and would not stop. He was astonished at the speed with which she covered the ground, the skill with which she avoided obstacles.

The great heavy cloak impeded him, and the crown threatened to slip from his head, but he would not abandon them. He held the cloak as best he could with his left hand, and the crown with his right, and kept running and calling. The dignity he had had when he first put them on was gone.

This thought suddenly struck him, then another. Why did he not leave her? He had rescued her from her tormenters and she must surely be grateful for that. But that was enough.

He had other things to do now, and would be better off without her.

'What things?' he asked himself.

He stopped running and adjusted the cloak carefully about him, and straightened the crown upon his head. He was in the robes of the Dark Lord, which, for some reason, had been left for him. Surely it was not by chance he had found them in this isolated place? He thought again of the crown that had so upset Glidd. Now he understood many things. He was a child of the Dark Star and Glidd and Firilla had spent all their time trying to keep this from him. But he was no ordinary vassal of a lord. The crown and cloak had been left for him.

He looked out over the darkening scene and smiled triumphantly. It was his time. The time of his power. For the first time he was not afraid of the dark.

From her hiding place behind a rock, Vallida watched him preening and tears came to her eyes. She saw him straighten his shoulders and turn away from her, striding off towards the west, towards Bar-geda.

She put her head to her knees and sobbed. She was utterly alone again. The cold night wind rustled the dry bushes and tugged at her clothes and she began to shiver uncontrollably. The cold of the crystal building, the fear of the Voices, the loneliness of having no personal existence, seemed nothing now to the cold, the fear and the loneliness of complete freedom.

Who could she turn to? No one. No one but herself. She stopped crying. Herself? Why not? 'The first thing I must do is to think calmly,' she told herself. 'And the first thing I need is shelter from this wind.'

She looked around her. Bardek was no longer in sight. The landscape was in no way as bleak as the desert plains they had travelled through before, but they had not yet reached the rich farmlands Bardek had told her about. There were no houses, and there was now very little light left from the dying Red Star.

She began to walk towards the horizon of Star rise, for no reason except that she had to move in some direction or freeze to death where she stood, and Star rise seemed a hopeful direction. She did not want to follow Bardek, although her heart ached for him. He would find her if he needed her, and if he did not need her it were best he did not find her.

She lifted her outer skirt of silk and held it over her head and shoulders like a cloak, glad that silk, though light, was warm and that she had two layers of it in her skirt, though her arms and shoulders were bare. She walked briskly, trying not to think of the dangers of her plight, stumbling from time to time on loose pebbles, bumping into larger rocks as the darkness deepened.

But through all this a small spark of something she had never felt before began to grow. A feeling so beautiful and light it almost lifted her off the ground. Where she should have been worrying about the possibilities of falling and breaking her neck, or being devoured by a wild beast, or starving or freezing to death, she was in fact feeling more and more confident and happy. For the first time in her life she was doing things for herself, thinking for herself, being herself. The Voices she so dreaded had not manifested in any way since Bardek had left and now she felt that something had happened inside her that would make it difficult for them to enter again. She had accepted responsibility for herself.

Bardek had felt compelled to put on the crown, and had accepted the compulsion. She had allowed herself to be used by the Voices, because her fear had made her believe deep inside that they had a right to use her. She had accepted them.

It would not happen again. She had a door she could lock against them, and the door was the knowledge she now had about herself.

She reached a rise in the ground and climbed to the top, looking upwards at the dark sky spattered with distant white sparks of light. Somewhere up there was the Dark Star, invisible, malevolent and sombre. 'No,' she suddenly thought, 'the Dark Star is not up there.'

She recalled the star map she had looked at. Her heart almost stopped beating with the shock of the revelation that had suddenly come to her: there was no Dark Star. It was an invention of the Voices.

Memories of things that had been said through her came crowding into her mind. The confidence and joy she had been feeling left her. The Dark Star might not exist but the Voices had a reality she could not dismiss. They no longer controlled her, but had they found another vessel? Bardek?

She lowered her eyes from the sky. Far to the south she saw lights glimmering at ground level. She began to walk towards them, finding it difficult to make progress over the uneven ground in the dark, but determined nevertheless to do so. Sometimes one of the lights disappeared as a rise in the ground or a line of bushes obstructed her view, but she kept going, and eventually came to a place where she could see them quite clearly. One light in particular seemed nearer than the others, and it was towards that one she directed her weary feet. It proved to come from a cabin on the edge of the farming lands, a shepherd's shieling. She looked through the window and saw a very old man sitting by a hearth fire.

She tapped loudly at the door and the old man looked up, alert, but did not move. She tapped again and called out loudly that she needed shelter, and this time she heard a wooden chair scrape on a wooden floor and footsteps slowly coming nearer. But they stopped in front of the door and the old man made no move to open it.

'I mean you no harm,' she called out. 'I am alone, cold and hungry. Please help me.'

At this he drew the bolt and opened the door. The light from inside the cabin blazed out and dazzled her. She shaded her eyes with her hand and blinked at him.

He had been prepared for a woman by her voice, but he had not been prepared for such a woman. Although her dress was torn and stained and dusty the silk still glowed softly and richly in the light that fell on her from inside the cabin, accentuating her beauty, her delicacy, her silver hair.

He stared at her for a few moments in silence, then stood back and indicated she should enter. He didn't take his eyes off her as she crossed the dusty floor and came to rest in front of his meagre hearth fire.

'I'm sorry if I startled you,' she said gently, 'but I was lost in the wilderness and if I'd stayed out for much longer I would have died.' With the last words came a tremor in her voice, and the strength that had kept her going deserted her. She sank to a low stool beside the fire and wept. How often in the past she had longed to die to free herself of her masters, but now that she was free the longing to live had become her master.

The old man hobbled to her side. 'I have some broth, and bread. You must eat.'

She nodded, but could not speak.

He brought her a bowl of broth scooped out of a big black pot that stood by the side of the fire, and tore off a piece of bread from a loaf that lay amongst a mess of things on a rickety table. She ate hungrily, but she could not relax. At the back of her mind two things were bothering her. One was that the old man looked at her as though he recognised her; the other was her anxiety for Bardek. Their roles had been reversed, and it was now he who needed her. But physical weariness got the better of her and with the warmth from the fire and the food inside her she soon found she could not keep her eyes open.

When she woke she found the old man had tidied up the room in her honour, and had cooked a meal of vegetables and meat.

'Are you a shepherd?' she asked as she sat in the chair he placed for her.

'I used to be,' he smiled, 'amongst other things.'

'What other things?' He hesitated and looked at her shrewdly as though weighing up how much he could trust her. 'You can trust me,' she said softly.

'I was once a priest. My name is Bar-Melchis.'

She looked at him, startled. 'I thought that once you were

a priest you were a priest until you died.'

He smiled, 'And I thought that once you were the Oracle, you were the Oracle until you died.'

'You know?' she said, strangely unalarmed.

He nodded.

'How?'

'I have not seen you since you were a very small child, and I didn't recognise you when you were standing at the door . . . probably because I was not expecting you . . .'

'You were a priest of the White Star?'

'Yes,' he said quietly. 'But I began to question things I should not have questioned, understand things I should not have understood . . .'

'You too!' she cried. It was surprising how different he seemed now that she knew something more about him. How could she ever have mistaken him for a shepherd?

'We are all prisoners. It is only the noticing of it that makes it so painful.'

'Of the White Star?'

'No. The Star has no power over us. That is an illusion they want us to believe.'

'They?' Vallida hardly dared hope that there was someone in the world beside herself who felt the menace of those 'Others', those Voices. 'You said "they". Who are "they"?'

'You know.'

'I only partially know. I know they are not gods. Tell me who they are.'

'The Sleepers who control this planet with the power of their dreams.'

Vallida gasped. She had known they were human, but had not imagined they might be asleep.

'Since man first came to this planet in the ancient times, there have been many changes,' Bar-Melchis said. 'The original colonists were those who had lived through a period of horror and chaos on the planet Earth that would be inconceivable to us now. They were the last to leave before its destruction, and they left enclosed in sleeping capsules. When they landed on Agaron they woke. They found the planet revolved around a sun, the White Star, and had five large moons. They started a colony, but, because they themselves had not changed, they found they were recreating on this planet the very conditions that had destroyed Earth. A few had sufficient intelligence to realise what was happening. They met in secret to plan a New Order for Agaron, an Order that could be imposed only because the colony was still so small and closely knit and had not then reached the level of Earth corruption, Earth violence.'

Vallida listened intently. He spoke with great authority.

'One of the techniques that had been developed, and misused, on Earth before the end was that of dream control . . .'

'Dream control? Sleepers?' she murmured.

'There was a legend in a place called Greece on Earth that when the new gods, Zeus and the Olympians, began their reign, they banished the old, the Titans of the Golden Age. Atlas was turned to stone and became a mountain holding up the sky; Prometheus was bound to a rock; Cronos was banished to an island in the western seas and imprisoned in eternal sleep. With him were his attendants, who received his dream commands and passed them on to the rest of the world.'

Vallida shivered, suddenly sensing something of the immensity of the web of existence in which she was caught – the threads that wove her life were the same that wove the lives of all who lived in time and space no matter how long ago or far away . . .

'Quite early on it had been discovered that people could influence other people with their thoughts, but most effectively while they were asleep and their conscious minds relaxed their vigilance. Later it was found that it was possible, like Cronos, for the dreams of a trained sleeper to influence the thoughts of a subject fully awake. The group that met on Agaron had worked on this technique on Earth, where it had been used to bring about the mental breakdown of enemies. Here on Agaron they planned to use it for a very

159

different purpose. They intended to escape from the violence and evil of waking life into the 'safe' context of controlled dreaming, and from there, themselves uninfluenced by the pressure of external events, impose by a kind of hypnotic projection a stability and order on the community that otherwise it would not have had.'

'How do you know all this?' cried Vallida, almost dizzy with the thoughts that were crowding into her head with his words. 'A priest of the White Star cannot have access to such things.'

'A High Priest can,' Bar-Melchis said drily. 'He has access to the most secret records. None of my predecessors had bothered to read them. But when I started thinking for myself, questioning and puzzling, I decided to open the silver box that contained the records and try to decipher them. It was there I learned that the six original colonists who had made the decision shut themselves away in their sleeping capsules, connected to the life support system they had arrived with, and simply went to sleep.'

'You mean . . .'

'That our whole planet and the people on it are being influenced without knowing it by the dreams of those six. The gods whom we believe are linked with the Stars are those same six.'

'I knew it!' she cried excitedly. 'I knew the Voices were not the voices of real gods! The Oracle must be the mouthpiece of the Sleepers when they want to communicate more directly! But . . . you said six of the colonists shut themselves away. Yet we have seven gods.'

'The seventh does not exist, even as a Sleeper. The six dream in turn, triggered by some pre-arranged signal linked to the 'Stars' of Agaron. The influence of each Star is different because each Sleeper is different. But the seventh dream casket is empty. There is no Dark Star. There is no Dark Lord.'

Vallida was triumphant. That was something else she had worked out for herself.

'They decided to leave one period blank, without control, as a kind of monitor of man as he is in his natural state without control. Only of course it is not his 'natural' state but the state he had come to through millennia of misusing the gift of life on Earth.'

'So the disorder and evil that seem to rule during the time of the Dark Star is brought about by the withdrawal of the Sleepers' dreams at that time?'

Bar-Melchis nodded.

'But why invent a Dark Lord at all? Why not just leave the time a blank?'

'Because the Sleepers in the early stages were trying to establish the control of authority and did not want people to know even for a moment that they could be free to make their own decisions.'

It all made sense, but there was still a great deal that worried Vallida. 'But if what you say is true . . .' she said thoughtfully.

'It is true.'

'The Sleepers and their dreams are good because they have made an orderly society out of chaos.'

'Yes.'

'But . . .'

'But?'

'Why did you rebel against them? Why did I?'

'Aha!' he cried, delighted that she had asked this question, transformed now from the ragged old man she had first seen to a lively, active-minded, ageless person. 'Because what should have been no more than a temporary emergency measure has become locked into a perpetual system, and the Sleepers' dreams are now a negative rather than a positive factor. Generations have gone by since the colonisation, and gradually the period of the Dark Star, the period of no control, has become less brutal, less violent. People are becoming capable of self-control, of natural kindness and concern towards their fellows, as they used to be on Earth before those terrible last days. But if these capabilities are not allowed to develop naturally by being used in a free situation they might well shrivel and disappear again. I tried to tell my fellow priests, but they would not listen.'

'It seems to me,' Vallida said with conviction, 'now that we know all this, we ought to do something about it.'

'If I knew what to do I would do it.'

'If we were to wake the Sleepers . . .'

'Ah, that is what we *should* do. But I do not know where the Sleepers are.'

'The records . . .'

'The records did not say. Perhaps they deliberately left that piece of information out, not wanting to be found, not wanting to be woken. Perhaps their intent was good . . .'

'If we were to go to Bar-geda, to the Temple of the Blue Star – my mother, the High Priestess, tried to help me – perhaps the priestesses would know something.'

Bar-Melchis looked thoughtful. 'It is possible the Sleepers divided the records between the two most important Temples, keeping them separate so that no one person could master all the information at one time. It is possible . . .' His voice trailed away.

Vallida was already standing up, eager to leave.

'It has been a long time,' Bar-Melchis muttered. 'A long time.'

'All the more reason to start at once,' Vallida said quickly. 'Everything is in confusion now. It will be easier to knock the whole thing off balance.'

The old man looked at her, torn between alarm and elation. He hesitated for a few moments, then stood up. 'Your name,' he said, 'means Truth. I will take it as a sign.'

He bustled about and found her a warm cloak. Then he flung his own over his shoulders, lit a torch at the fire, and, holding it like a beacon above his head, walked out into the dark.

With heart beating fast, Vallida followed him.

CHAPTER 14

The Dark Lord

When Bardek left Vallida he had no clear purpose. He knew only that he had a sense of power and that the urge to return to Bar-geda was strong. Was he destined to bring about great changes? Had he not already brought about great changes?

He strode easily through the darkness, hardly feeling his fatigue. He was convinced the Dark Lord had chosen him for some great work and was helping him even in the simple matter of covering the ground between himself and the city. He was sure that when he arrived it would be made clear to him what it was he had to do.

Strangely, he did not think of Vallida at all, but his mother came to mind, and he knew how upset she would be that he was now wearing the mantle of the Dark Star and serving its Lord.

Serving the Dark Lord?

He rejected the idea. He wore the cloak and the crown of the Master, which had been specially left for him. Had he not taken over the role of the Dark Lord? Was he not himself the Dark Lord? The significance of this thought thrilled him. He tried to tell himself that to think like this was crazy, that he was Bardek of the mountains, son of Firilla, but a sly voice in his head pointed out that he had been told he was the son of Firilla, as he had been told he was conceived under the Green and born under the Red, but he knew now that that was not true. Child of the Dark Star? He was proud of it. He thought his motive in overthrowing the White Temple had been to rescue the girl he loved from suffering; but now he wondered if he had even then been guided by his destiny to break the power of the White Lord by removing the channel through which he gave his commands.

An image of the girl flashed through his mind and a twinge of his old feeling for her stirred, but he set it aside at once. He had duties and obligations. The Skull still existed and while it did it seemed the Oracle could still be used. The priesthood of the White Temple was crippled by the destruction of their crystal edifice; the most powerful priesthood left was the one that served the Blue Star. It had been their High Priestess who had helped him to overthrow the Skull, and it was possible that her successor would be prepared to tell him more about the Skull and where it now was.

It was to the Blue Temple he must go.

Firilla and Glidd sat on the floor of the chamber of the Sleepers, propped against the wall. His arms were around her, his mind struggling to think of a way out of the trap they were in, trying not to think of the hunger pains he was suffering. Firilla had fallen asleep, her head nestled into his shoulder, the lines of anxiety on her forehead gradually disappearing as she relaxed. He thought of the people in the caskets and wondered how long they had been there. As far as the boy understood it was 'since the beginning of time'. He had told them that when he was very small his grandparents had been the Servants, then his parents had taken over. When he was questioned he remembered his grandfather had spoken of his own grandfather. The Sleepers had lain in their caskets, mysteriously kept alive, unchanged, while generations of prisoners in this chalk cave served them, having no life but to turn knobs and eat pills. How monstrous!

That the caskets so precisely corresponded to the colours of the Stars had not escaped him. It was clear that the Sleepers were intimately connected with the Star Lords. Perhaps they were the gods themselves.

Glidd sighed and his head ached. These figures, human

as himself, dreaming away the aeons at the expense of others' lives, were not what he expected or wanted the gods to be. He called the boy over. 'Do they ever speak?' he whispered. The boy shook his head. 'Have they ever done anything in all your memory, except lie there and dream?' Again Servant shook his head.

Glidd's thoughts turned and turned on the implications of what he had seen in the chamber, weariness and hunger dulling his mind. He began to remember how once, as a child . . . when his parents died . . . he had longed to go to sleep and never wake up. Now as he looked at Firilla he wondered if they could both dream out the last part of their lives and not notice the gradually increasing pangs of hunger and the fear of dying. Something in the movement of her eyes told him she was already dreaming. If only he could join her and they could journey together far from this cold mortuary for the living to some place where there were mountains and feathered whains singing in the dawn of the White Star . . .

His lids began to feel heavy and his cheek lowered until it rested on Firilla's hair. A voice began to speak in his head . . . at first from a great distance, gradually getting nearer. It was telling him a story . . . he was a child listening to a story . . .

'Atman was given the secret of the universe as a gift. He was pleased, but he didn't know what to do with it. At first he tested it in all kinds of ways to find out what it was, but failing to get a satisfactory answer he played with it as though it were a bauble or a toy. Eventually he hung it on a tree as decoration. And then he forgot it.

So it stayed for a long time . . . an unconsidered trifle . . . until one day someone came by who recognised it and asked if he might have it.

Atman gladly parted with it in exchange for an artefact and went off satisfied that he had struck a good bargain, rejoicing in his newly acquired treasure.

The one who now had the secret of the universe saw that it was a seed and planted it in his garden. It grew to be the Tree of Life and he sat in its shade in the heat of the day and was filled with great reverence and love.

All things were clear to him.

All things were good.

Meanwhile Atman began to grow dissatisfied and miserable. The artefact no longer pleased him. He was bored with it. He had done whatever there was to be done with it on the first day and thereafter he could find out nothing new about it.

The man who had the Secret of the Universe however was never bored, its variations were infinite, his interest in it ever deepening.

At last Atman, having realised his mistake, came to the man and asked for it back. But now the price was so high Atman could not pay it.

He went away and worked for endless aeons to earn the price of the thing he had sold so carelessly and so cheaply before. 'When I get it back,' he thought, 'I will never let it go, for indeed, it is the only thing worth having.'

At that moment the man standing under the Tree of Life reached out to him and gave him freely of its fruit.'

Glidd woke with a jerk. The voice that had been telling the story ceased. His strange and compelling dream was over and he was back in the chamber of the Sleepers. It had seemed to him that he had been on another planet, a planet called Earth. During the dream he had not questioned the existence of the Atman or the Tree of Life; it had all seemed perfectly clear.

The dream world he longed to enter with Firilla before he had fallen asleep had been, he realised, an escape from reality. But this dream had been no escape, rather an entering into Reality. He felt he had been given a message of great importance. But from whom?

He looked at the Sleepers, but he knew that it was not from any of them.

He was now wide awake, every sense alert, no longer troubled by hunger or thirst. Gently he put Firilla's sleeping body aside and started to stride about the chamber.

Servant was asleep on his little couch beside the caskets. Glidd alone was awake. He alone was thinking, with a mind clearer than it had ever been. He looked at the screens. The line on each of them registered a mild dream state. It was the time of the empty casket, the Dark Lord, and nothing registered there.

The Secret of the Universe? What was it?

What was it?

He paced up and down, up and down the confined space. If he understood his dream he would be free, of that he was sure. He had never had a dream like it. It was as though for the first time, while it lasted, he was awake, and all the rest of his life he had been asleep.

When Bardek reached Bar-geda he strode straight through the deserted dark streets to the Blue Temple. He found it glowing quietly in the long night of the Dark Star; translucent, seemingly floating in the air like some exquisite cluster of luminescent bubbles. He looked across the city to where the temple of white crystal had once stood, half expecting it to have been raised again. But he could see nothing.

He hurried towards the Blue Temple, avoiding the patrols of guardians, somehow unnoticed in his dark mantle. They carried torches but their light barely lifted the shadow of the Dark Star from their own heads, let alone from the street around them, and Bardek could sense both their fear and their uneasiness.

He stood in the shadows for a long while, watching the gatekeeper of the Blue Temple, and carefully chose his moment to move in behind her as silently as darkness itself. As he seized her by the neck she gave no more than a sigh as she slipped unconscious to the ground, the alarm unsounded.

Boldly he strode up the path and the wide stairs to the entrance. Enormous columns flanked a gigantic studded silver door. He had found no keys on the woman and presumed therefore that the door would be guarded but unlocked. He was wrong. The place was deserted and the door immovable.

'I'll not be foiled now,' he muttered angrily, and started to beat his fists against the door. He beat until his arms ached, but no one appeared in the vast antechamber he could just dimly see through the crystal walls. He cursed, he kicked the polished silver and then . . . he paused to think.

Negg had given him a small piece of hollow reed with holes in it when they were making their way out of the marshes and shown him how to make music with it. Bardek had played for a while and then had forgotten about it. He reached into his pocket and pulled it out. It was slightly battered but still usable. Firilla used to say that no knowledge was ever wasted, that what seemed irrelevant at one time became relevant at another. Now was the time for his knowledge of the reed. He fitted it to the keyhole and blew with all the breath in his body. A wild and fearsome melody, magnified by the vast keyhole, reverberated in the hall beyond. Louder and louder he blew until figures began to emerge from the corridors beyond and rush into the antechamber, confused, looking everywhere for the source of the amazing sound.

When Bardek could see that the room was full of people he replaced the reed and spoke directly into the keyhole, imitating the Lady Maya's voice. 'Open the door! Your Lady commands it!'

His voice, like the voice of the reed, was magnified and distorted eerily. Horrified, the women stared at the door.

'Open!'

They looked at each other in frightened bewilderment for a moment, and then a few rushed to do his bidding while others shouted that they should not and tried to hold them back.

As the huge silver leaves of the door rolled open, Bardek strode into the chamber. The women screamed and retreated.

Was it the Dark Lord himself? His eyes were fiercely triumphant, his black cloak swirled as he moved, the crown of garrar feathers was tall upon his head, its obsidian and ruby flashing and glinting malevolently.

They ran. Bardek followed, rightly assuming they would rush to tell the High Priestess. Somewhere deep inside his own voice tried to raise objection to the role he was playing, but he ignored it. He had never felt so exhilarated.

He arrived in the hall of the blue sapphire throne under the highest dome in time to see the High Priestess rush into the hall, still pushing her hair up into its crown of blue feathers, the ribbons of her robe only half clothing her. He strode swiftly across the floor and positioned himself at the foot of the stairs so that her way to the throne was blocked.

She stopped breathlessly in front of him, caught off guard, her face as confused as any ordinary woman's would have been.

'What! Did you not foresee this visit, prophetess?'

She did not answer. He could see her breast moving up and down as her breath came short. He could see fear in her eyes. Fear of him!

She was a beautiful woman, and in that moment he desired her. But she was already beginning to pull herself together.

'Stand aside, Dark Lord,' she said haughtily. 'This is the throne room of the High Priestess of the Blue Star. You have no right to be here.'

'I have what rights I have the strength to take.' He saw fear flicker in her eyes momentarily, but she controlled it.

'You misunderstand the nature of things, my lord. To take by force is to lose. To be given is to keep.'

'You will give what I ask for, then.'

She laughed bitterly. 'I will not.'

He was angry that she dared laugh, that the fear had gone out of her eyes. He strode forward and took her by the arms.

169

The women in the hall gasped, but none moved forward to help.

She tipped back her head and met his fierce stare with a steady blue gaze. 'What now, my lord? Will you rape me?'

He bit his lip. He dropped her arms. What was he doing? He suddenly became aware of his own state of confusion. Who was he? As Dark Lord he wanted to destroy the Skull in order to end the power of the White priests. As Bardek he wanted to destroy the Skull in order to free Vallida. Yet here he was being distracted from both aims by a mixture of anger and desire for a woman who meant nothing to him. For a moment he felt he was back in the marshes struggling through the mist, not knowing where he was or where he was going. He was not in charge of himself. He was being used. He was slipping into the identity of the Dark Lord one moment and out of it the next. Again he recalled the marshes, where he had the experience of being in several places at once.

He shook his head violently as though trying to free it of something that was invisible to the others.

'No, my lady,' he said at last. 'I want information.'

'And will you ask for it, my lord?'

'I will.'

'Then if it is in my power to give, I will give it to you.'

Bardek stepped aside and started to pace up and down at the foot of the stair. With a curt movement of her hand Kirini indicated that the priestesses and novices present should move back. She herself took her stand on the second step so that she was just a shade taller than him. She watched him pace, fully in control of herself now. Her crown was properly in place, the ribbons of her gown falling where they should.

Back and forth Bardek paced. Back and forth.

'There is a skull, my lady, made of crystal,' he said at last, coming to rest in front of her, looking into her eyes.

'A skull, my lord?'

'A giant skull from the Temple of the White Star.' She gave no indication that she knew what he was talking about, but looked at him with cool appraisal, waiting for him to continue. 'It used to stand in the Great Hall.'

'Used to stand?'

He could not quite place the intonation of her voice. Was it mockery, or genuine surprise at the implications of the question?

'Yes, used to, my lady.'

'I think you will find, my lord, that it is still there.'

'It is not. I myself knocked it from its plinth and saw it buried in the debris of the Temple.'

'Then it has been replaced,' she said sharply. 'There is nothing you can do of lasting harm, Lord of the Dark Star, against the power of the god of Light.'

'His Temple is destroyed. I have destroyed it!' Bardek said, coldly, furiously.

'I think not, my lord.'

He lifted his hand to strike her, incensed that she belittled his power. But at that moment there was a disturbance at the door and he, with the others, turned his attention towards it.

Two people entered. One, an old, ragged man leaning on a stick, the other a young girl of astonishing beauty, white silk flowing around her, silver hair an aura around her head.

'Vallida!' his heart cried out to her as though it were a trapped creature calling for deliverance. But the tall and imposing figure standing in the long cloak beneath the sapphire throne said nothing.

The women who should have tried to hold intruders back fell aside and bowed to the ground at the sight of the girl.

Bardek was enough himself to note that the lost, wondering, bewildered look she had had when he first released her into the world was gone. She swept across the hall through the bowed women like a queen among her subjects. 'Bardek,' she commanded, looking straight into his eyes, 'take off that crown!'

Was he to have no respect from anyone? He drew himself up to his full height and glared at her. 'Woman, you forget yourself!'

'No, Bardek . . . it is you who forget.' There was a touch of regret and tenderness in her voice, but she was nonetheless in control of herself.

'And who are you, my lady?' he said coldly, sarcastically.

For a moment the old suffering, the old insecurity, flickered across her face, but it was soon gone. 'My name is Vallida, sir, a woman who is now very well aware of who she is!'

'Where are your Voices, Oracle, to give you strength? Without your Voices you are nothing.'

If she suffered at his words she gave no sign. She stood straight and still, looking at him steadily. 'You are wrong, sir. *With* my Voices I was nothing, as you are now.'

'What? Nothing?'

'Yes, you are nothing. You have given up your own autonomy and the dreams of others speak through you.'

A flicker of uncertainty crossed his face. He suddenly remembered the woman who had held the burning branch in the marsh hut, and he had himself influenced the dreams of Negg. What was she saying?

The old man hobbled forward. 'You have all abandoned yourselves for a dream that is not even your own.'

Vallida swept her arm around to indicate the whole shimmering beauty of the hall, the magnificent stairway, the throne that shone. 'Will you not see how false this all is?' she demanded of the women crowding anxiously together. They moved forward, murmuring angrily. The eyes of the High Priestess sparked dangerously. 'Break free of the dream,' Vallida cried. 'Become what you were meant to be!'

'Do it now,' the old man said urgently, 'while there is darkness, for in darkness there are no dreams. You are free if you will only recognise it. When the next Star rises you will be under their complete control again.'

'Their?' Kirini snapped. 'What blasphemy do you speak, strangers? Are you aware of where you are? Seize them!' Angrily she gestured her women forward. They moved, emboldened by her words, ready to act.

'Stop!' Bar-Melchis had not forgotten how to command like a High Priest, how to transfix with the power of thought and eye. 'You will listen, lady, and call off your hounds. What I have to tell you is the most important thing you have ever heard.'

'Seize them!' said Bardek suddenly. 'Destroy them!'

'Ah, my lord,' said Kirini, holding up her hand to stop the advance of her women. 'They are not your children then? Hold. Let them speak. The girl is surely the Oracle of the White Lord, and the old man speaks with an authority I recognize, though I do not know his name.'

Full of rage Bardek took a step forward as though he would himself silence the old man if the priestess would not.

Bar-Melchis looked into his eyes.

He had lived alone a long time and the power he now had in his gaze was as much from the strength of his own wisdom as from the training he had received to become High Priest.

Bardek wavered.

'Listen to me, Bardek of the mountains. Listen to me all you who think you serve the Lady of the Blue Star . . .'

'Think?' cried Kirini angrily.

But in spite of their anger the women found themselves listening to the old man's words, each one he spoke sinking deeper and deeper into their consciousness until they found they could fight them no more.

'There are Sleepers, Dreamers, who rule this planet. You call them gods, but they are no more godlike than you are.' There was an angry murmur at this, but it was like thunder from a spent storm.

'My mother, your predecessor,' Vallida interrupted, speaking directly to Kirini, 'must have had her doubts, for she came to free me from the Temple of the White Star, and died in the attempt.'

The women crowded forward to listen, bewildered and anxious, not knowing what to think. Bardek stood momentarily forgotten, frowning in concentration. If there were no dreams at the time of the Dark Star and yet she had said that he was under the influence of someone else's dream at the moment . . .

Vallida must have caught his thought, for she turned to him and took his hands in hers, looking most earnestly and lovingly into his eyes. 'The Sleepers imbue everything with their dreams,' she explained, 'and it is difficult for us to sort out which of our experiences are our own and which are theirs. Most, I think, are a mixture of both. The crown you found, and the cloak, do not belong to the Dark Lord, for there is no Dark Lord. But because the Sleepers have led us to believe there is one, you took the trappings of his power and put them on, deceiving yourself even when the Sleepers were not directly influencing you. You see how necessary it is for us to break away now,' she said gently, 'before we lose all hope of independence?'

Bardek dropped his hands and turned away, full of shame. There was silence for a moment as they all looked at him, pondering on what they had heard. And then Bar-Melchis began to speak again. He told them all he knew of Earth and the early times on Agaron, and how the Sleepers had enforced order upon chaos, which once had been for the good of their kind but which now had outlived its usefulness and was keeping them back from developing as they should. 'How can a muscle develop if it is not used? How can a conscience, a sense of right and wrong, be developed if it is never tested?'

He told them that the original Sleepers would not survive much longer. They had programmed themselves for a certain time span.

'Will we be free then?' Kirini asked, reluctant to believe this incredible revelation, yet knowing that there were things in it that made sense for the first time of experiences she herself had had.

'No. For they have worked out their programme so carefully that they will cease to dream only when their dreams are no longer necessary — that is, when we are so conditioned that we cannot change our ways of thinking and acting even without them. We become self-perpetuating puppets . . . Look at Bardek there. He thinks he is the Dark Lord not because they are dreaming him as the Dark Lord but because he is responding to a symbol they have conditioned him to respond to.'

'What is to be done then?' cried Kirini. She was becoming more and more convinced of the truth of what he said.

'If we could wake them before the programme is complete, before the final condition . . .' He was interrupted by a sudden crashing sound. Everyone looked round to find that Bardek had ripped the crown from his head and sent it spinning across the floor until it broke apart against one of the fluted columns.

He tore the mantle from his shoulders and sent it flying after the crown.

They could see by the agony on his face that it had taken a supreme act of will to divest himself of the powerful image.

Vallida ran to him. 'O my love,' she cried. 'Now we have hope.'

He held her close, shivering with the strain of the conflict he had just won.

'But if you are right,' said Kirini, 'where are the Sleepers we must wake?'

The old man shook his head. 'We had hoped you would have records . . .'

Kirini looked despairing. 'Only the Temple of the White Star had records.'

'And those were incomplete,' said Bar-Melchis sadly.

'What of the Skull?' Bardek lifted his head from Vallida's hair, his own thoughts returning to him. 'The Skull is some kind of key to all this. You said it was back at the White Temple?' He looked at Kirini, who nodded. 'If it is there we must go then – all of us.'

'All of us?' cried Kirini. It was unthinkable for the priestesses of the Temple to run about the streets like ordinary people.

'All of us,' said Vallida firmly. 'And quickly, before the Blue Star rises.'

The mention of the Blue Star recalled the High Priestess to her duties. 'I cannot miss the Rising,' she said in alarm. 'Without the proper rituals . . .'

'You see – there is your conditioning!'

'But . . .'

'There is no time to lose,' Vallida urged.

'But what if chaos returns . . . you have no guarantee . . .'

'Believe me,' Bar-Melchis interrupted. 'I am an old man. I have seen much, and I can tell you there are signs that show me we are capable of being real people making our own decisions again. For a long time the period of the Dark Star has not been so violent as it used to be. Vallida has told me of two marsh dwellers who helped save her life. People are starting to question things. Bardek, before he fell victim to the symbol of power, was thinking for himself . . .'

'Nevertheless, I cannot go,' the High Priestess said. 'If you are wrong, or if you fail, I will be here to keep the net of order tight around the planet. If you are right, I wish you good fortune. If you are successful, then when the Sleepers are awakened I will give you all the help I can . . . for there will still be much to do before we grow used to the new order.'

'We cannot ask for more than that,' Bar-Melchis said quietly. 'Good fortune go with you too my lady.'

CHAPTER 15

Release

When Bardek, Vallida and Bar-Melchis came within sight of the hill on which they expected to find only the ruins of the White Temple, they were amazed to see that there was a simple crystal structure raised in place of the previous complexity.

They started to scramble up the slope, now full of broken crystal and uprooted trenoids, but Bar-Melchis found that he could not stand the pace. He called to the two young people that they should go ahead and let him follow when he could. Most of his life he had waited for this moment, and he was now sorely afraid it had come too late for him. His chest ached and his breath came short as he tried to climb the hill. But he was determined to survive. As each pain came that warned him he must not push his heart too far he rested until it passed, and then struggled a little further, sometimes on his hands and knees. He had never been particularly afraid of death, but now he did not want to die until he had seen the end of what he had begun, and the beginning of what was to take its place.

He was sitting, panting, on a slab of rock, when Bardek and Vallida reached the top, turned, waved briefly to him and disappeared. He knew they were in great danger. The Sleepers were no ordinary sleepers, nor their Dreams ordinary dreams. And the Skull . . . Even he with all his knowledge did not know all there was to know about the Skull.

The new construction seemed to consist of just one totally transparent hall or box glowing in the dark, in the centre of which was a plinth. On the plinth was the Skull, not a scratch or a crack to show that it had fallen.

Vallida shuddered as she saw it and turned away. Bardek put his arm around her. 'Would you rather go back to Bar-Melchis and wait? I will tackle this alone.'

'No,' she said, and looked back at the Skull. It was alone, no longer attended by priests, but already she could feel the old dread returning, the draining away of the self-confidence she had so newly won. She shivered. How much longer had the Sleepers programmed themselves to sleep, and would she ever be able to tell which were her own thoughts and beliefs, and those 'dreamed' into her by others? Perhaps all that was happening was only a dream . . .

'I love you!' Bardek said suddenly, and kissed her long and deeply. She put her arms round his neck and clung to him. She could find no words to tell him how much what he had said meant to her; not so much the words he had used but the expression in his eyes as he said them and the communication of his lips as he kissed her. She could tell! She could tell what was real and what was not. What they would both have given to keep that moment just as it was, clear of all the bad memories and the fears for the future. But it could not be. They could almost feel the hollow eyes of the Skull upon them and, shuddering, drew apart.

There was no way in or out of the new structure, but Bardek confidently tried to think his way in again, holding Vallida close, and concentrating complete awareness on one crystal face, seeing what was apparently solid as a closely woven net of energy. But he remained frustratingly outside, and the Skull within.

He rested, sitting wearily on the low wall that edged the basin where a fountain had once played. Bar-Melchis joined them at last, at first unable to speak, his chest heaving too much with the effort of the climb.

When they told him the problem he gazed at the Skull for a long time. 'You have both tried mind-energy and bodily force, and neither has had effect. We must think of another way.'

'I think,' said Vallida, 'it is for me to try. I was – am – the Oracle, who gave the lifeless Skull a tongue. I must be the one to challenge it now.'

'No!' Bardek cried.

'She is right,' Bar-Melchis told him with quiet authority, and Bardek fell silent.

Already she was moving away from them, her mind withdrawn from them.

'Vallida.' Bardek tried to rise and go after her, but the old man touched his arm and held him back.

She walked straight ahead quite boldly, and without hesitation she passed through the wall as though it was not there. Bardek leapt up at once and tried to rush after her, but the hard crystal she had penetrated apparently so easily resisted him. He began to beat on the walls passionately, despairingly, but she took no notice.

She walked across the white marble floor gracefully, calmly, and stood in front of the plinth. The Skull was on the same level as her own and she looked directly into its eye sockets.

When she fought this formidable adversary before it had been because she did not understand what was happening to her. She had feared it and resented it. Now she chose deliberately, of her own will, to face it, and it was a very different situation. In the past when she had stared into the blank, transparent holes of the crystal eye sockets she had begun to feel as though something cold and strange was entering her body, and then she would hear the Voices shouting from her own mouth. No matter how much she had resented what was about to happen to her, or how much she struggled to prevent it, sooner or later she had given in. But now she was stronger, and when she began to feel the eerie power invading her mind she told herself it was only the Sleepers, humans like herself, who were transmitting their dream voices through her, using the inanimate Skull as a kind of transformer.

'No,' she said firmly. 'This time I will not be your medium. It is *I* who will speak to you.'

She was determined not to be afraid. She had found confidence in her own Self since she last encountered the Voices. Bar-Melchis had said that her name meant Truth, and truth would now be her weapon. Her shield would be her love for Bardek, and his for her. She was going to free herself and her world once and for all if she died in the attempt.

Waves of cold passed over her, but she kept staring boldly into the hollow eyes.

'You are nothing,' she said. 'Nothing. You are the construction of a dream, whereas I have my own reason for being, and my own source of consciousness dependent on no other!'

As she said the words and realised the truth of them she could feel the beginning of victory, but just at that moment she was distracted by a shout from Bardek.

'Hurry!' he called. She looked over her shoulder at him. In that moment her adversary gained ground.

She screamed suddenly and held her head. That horrible, familiar feeling was creeping under her hair, causing her skin to prick and her heart to drain of hope.

Bardek saw her go rigid, saw her lift her arms, saw her open her mouth to utter words that were not her own.

Deep beneath the Temple of the White Star, Glidd watched over Firilla. She was deathly pale. There were three pills left in Servant's dispenser: when the fourth had been ready to fall he had tried to seize it for Firilla, but the boy had tricked him and he had lost it.

He sat with his back against the wall with her in his arms, a feeling of great helplessness and despair in his heart. He could feel that she was slipping from him. In a little while she would be dead. In a little while they would both be dead. The boy with his three pills would be the last to go. And then . . . what?

How strange and brief and inexplicable life had become.

They had lived it as though it were going to last forever. Yet what had they understood of it? Very little. They had accepted what everybody believed and what they had been taught, but now, as he thought about it, no one had ever satisfactorily explained to him why he was alive, why he in particular was alive. Was this mystery the seed that grew into the Tree of Life? Was the great Secret of the Universe that Life is a Mystery and must remain a Mystery? The people of Earth, disregarding this, had tried to find certainty, tried to make everything explicable and controllable. No one looked for understanding, everyone looked for explanations. And so each leader, each scientist, each priest, having his own 'explanation' and implementing measures to enforce it on the rest of the human race, came in conflict with every other leader, scientist or priest who had another 'explanation'. And, as each explanation failed ultimately to explain, disillusionment and despair grew.

Now on Agaron, thought Glidd, the Sleepers had imposed their arbitrary explanation of life on the people, and the people had accepted it.

At that moment, realising that there was more to life than that which we can explain, Glidd understood that that 'more' was the gift that Atman had been given and had disregarded.

He did not know where Firilla and he had come from or where they were going . . . he did not know if there was even a journey on which they were engaged. And in that not knowing one way or the other lay the key to the secret of the universe. While the mystery remains we dare not kill our fellow men, we dare not destroy or exploit or maim. Who knows what greater justice we may have to face? Who knows what greater opportunity we are throwing away?

In the great clarity of mind Glidd was experiencing, perhaps because he was so near to death, he knew that the Sleepers were the gods they were supposed to worship. He knew the dreams they dreamed ruled the lives of those who walked on Agaron.

He gently disengaged himself from Firilla's frail body

and stood up. He felt very weak and very ill, but he had made a decision he was determined to implement. The Sleepers must be woken.

The boy was away from the chamber and Glidd's way was clear. He took his belt off and held the large metal buckle firmly in his right hand. Then he tried to prise the dial panel off the red casket. The crystal box was strong but the panel had been loosened slightly over the ages by frequent usage, and, first with his nails, then with the buckle, he managed to get purchase. He levered and pushed and fiddled until at last he could rip it off.

He staggered as it came free, and stared with horror into the casket. The figure of the Red Sleeper turned slowly, his face distorting with terrible agony and then, as Glidd watched, sickened, his whole body turned to dust.

Glidd jumped back and leant against the wall, shivering and trembling. He had intended to wake the Sleepers and make them stop dreaming so that the people of Agaron would be free. He had not expected this.

Even as he decided he must meddle no more and leave the other caskets untouched, the readings on the screens began to register severe disturbances: nightmare. Frantically Glidd turned knobs as he had watched Servant do, but the Sleepers did not respond. He had destroyed their careful balance and they were in shock. He didn't know what to do. If the Sleepers' dreams controlled the surface of the planet, their agitation must be wreaking havoc. Having destroyed one, he must destroy them all. He immediately started to work on the next casket.

The citizens of Bar-geda began to wake from sleep, screaming. The ground beneath their city was moving, houses were shaking, solid walls cracking and crumbling. This was a much more widespread groundquake than that which had destroyed the Temple of the White Star, too big to blame on the Children of the Dark Star.

* * * *

On the hill of the White Temple, Bardek was frantically trying to break into the hall of the Skull. Like a transparent box
it was being tilted this way and that with the shaking of the
ground, Vallida being tossed from side to side like a marble
in a child's toy, her body crashing time and again against the
hard walls.

Bar-Melchis had fallen to the ground when the shaking
started. He wept for the girl, because he could see that she
was being badly battered, and he wept for his world, which
was in the throes of either birth, or of death.

The sky was a mass of swirling dark cloud, illuminated
from time to time by deadly swords of light. One sliced the
darkness open and stayed so long it seemed as though the two
sides of the sky had been permanently sundered. In the crack
appeared a huge face, more fearsome than anything they had
ever imagined, its eyes blazing, its forked tongue as black as
obsidian, flickering in and out as though trying to lick up the
people running helplessly through the streets. Its breath was
like a wind from the desert plains of Marvara . . .

The dykes that Negg and Millon and a few of the marsh
dwellers had painstakingly built to defend themselves against
the expected vengeful raid of the city dwellers, were swept
aside by a sudden flood of water that was sucked up by the
hideous face and spewed out far and wide.

'Is this the Sleepers' nightmare, or our own?' thought Bar-
Melchis.

Beneath the city, Glidd worked feverishly to finish what he
had begun. The boy had returned and was horrified to see
what was happening. He rushed straight to the controls of

183

those caskets still unopened and tried to adjust the dream-patterns. But nightmare on such a scale was insanity and could not be controlled. He stood wringing his hands, staring as Glidd continued his terrible work. They could feel the ground shaking. The cavern that they had been trapped in was collapsing, the sound of it fearsomely loud in the chalk-walled chamber.

The third last pill was ejected, but neither Glidd nor the boy noticed it roll away across the floor. Firilla slumped forward, white dust shaken from the ceiling covering her with a fine film.

When they opened the blue casket the Temple of the Blue Star exploded into countless millions of shining blue dust particles. Kirini was on the sapphire throne staring out at the holocaust with wide and frightened eyes. It seemed to her that a bolt of livid blue lightning hit the peak of the dome above her and hovered there. And then, in slow motion, the building disintegrated. She was perfectly conscious as she fell, knowing that this was her death, but feeling no fear, nor even, to her momentary surprise, resentment. With extraordinary intensity of vision she saw the spiralling motes of blue and gold and silver that had once been a mighty edifice floating down with her.

The white casket was the most stubborn of all to open. Glidd was so weak and ill he could hardly stand, but he could not stop what he had started. Servant at last moved to help him, knowing that there was no going back. As the lid came off, the White Sleeper's face distorted with hate and rage, and it seemed for an instant that he would rise from the casket and rip them to pieces. But even as he began to move he fell to dust as the others had before him.

'If only they had woken!' sobbed Glidd. 'If only they had woken!'

He turned at last to Firilla, and found her in the dust, unconscious, very near to death. Sobbing, he took her in his arms.

'Come!' Servant cried urgently. 'Come – bring pretty lady – come!' He was beckoning from the doorway. They had both heard the roar as the roof of the cavern above them caved in, and could see the cracks appearing in their own ceiling as the weight of the fallen rock above and the shaking of the ground made even their deep strata unstable.

Not believing that there was anywhere to go, but his instinct for survival dominating him, Glidd lifted Firilla and ran after the boy. They sped down narrow passages of white chalk almost in total darkness as the torches that usually burned there had been shaken off the walls and sputtered out on the rock floor. They came at last to a chamber that must have been very deep underground and which mercifully was not reacting to the general quake. There they hid, starving, desperate, frightened, wondering if this would be their tomb . . .

On the hill of the White Temple the crystal box containing the Skull and Vallida had broken free and was lurching and sliding down the slope among the falling rocks and opening cracks, with Bardek scrambling frantically after it. He was aware of nothing but Vallida's danger and Vallida's pain. Her white silk dress was stained with blood as she was dashed against the walls. He could hear her screams as each new jolt flung her across the box. The Skull added another hazard as it broke free from its plinth and rolled about the chamber.

Suddenly there was a violent flash of light. As the last Sleeper disintegrated, his construct, the Skull, the transmitter of dreams, the channel of power, exploded into a myriad fragments, and with it the crystal box in which it was carried.

Bardek staggered back, almost blinded.

'Vallida!' he screamed. He could not live without her. He would not live without her! He stumbled forward, feeling in the dark, crying her name. He barely noticed that the ground had stopped shaking and the noise of the storm and wind had ceased. There was total silence. Total darkness. He bruised and cut his hands as he felt among the jagged rocks. A thought tormented him: had she ever existed as a real woman of flesh and blood? Was she too only a construct of the Sleepers' dreams?

In the darkness a light flickered beside him.

Bar-Melchis held the branch he had lit, and in the flame light he saw the young man's face streaked with dust and tears. He took his arm and pointed the light beyond him to where some trenoids had fallen ... Caught in a cradle of roots Vallida was lying, her dress tattered and stained, her skin broken and bruised, but stirring as though waking from a deep sleep.

Far away in the marshes, Negg and Millon surveyed the wreckage of the defence dykes they had been building. Many of the tribes-people who had been persuaded to help had been killed in the fearsome flood, but many, like Negg and Millon, were left clinging to the sledges that had been used to carry soil and rock from outside the marshes and which now served as rafts.

Negg looked round anxiously to see how many had survived. Everywhere he saw bodies, mud, the broken stems of reeds. But among that desolation he saw something else that even then, in that moment of despair, brought a lift to his heart: the survivors clinging together were of many different tribes, and those who helped others out of the water, and those who cried for help, were not looking to see what tribe rescuer or rescued came from.

When the next moon of Agaron, once known as the Blue Star, rose, it lit an extraordinary scene. There was no flashing mirror-stone orb to catch its beams in the dome of a beautiful crystal temple, but there were hundreds and thousands of sad and anxious eyes that lit with joy to greet its rising. One by one the seven hills of Bar-geda were bathed in its light, the city still in shadow, nursing its wounds, the survivors gathering in the stricken streets to watch the dawn, thinking of lost relatives, clutching the loved ones still alive close to them. Most of the casualties had been caused when a huge hole had opened in the centre of the city. People stood now at the edge staring at the darkness into which the Governors' Palace and many of the government buildings had collapsed. Around them were the seven hills on which no temple still stood. Their strange and invisible shackles had dropped from them, their 'gods' and the whole system of the Sleepers had in one horrifying night been destroyed. 'What now?' the people asked themselves, 'what now?'

It was Bardek who told them. It was Bardek who came down from the hill of the White Star and set them to work clearing the debris preparatory to rebuilding the houses.

He did not intend to be their leader but found that he could not help himself. They were so confused, so stunned, so unused to thinking for themselves. With the strength and wisdom of Bar-Melchis to guide him, and with the advantage of the awe people had for Vallida, he found himself making decisions and issuing orders.

So it was that on his order the people tried to salvage what they could from the great hole. In doing so they found the labyrinth of chalk tunnels below the city, and in a chamber off one of them, the remains of the Sleepers, and in another, deeper still, the bodies of Glidd and Firilla and a strange, wizened little boy.

Bardek stood looking down on them, his heart aching for love of them and for sorrow at his loss. What pleasure would he have in the rising of the white sun without Firilla's delight in it? How would he face the difficult times without Glidd's calm strength? Vallida touched his arm, and he buried his face in her hair and sobbed.

'We have to be strong,' she whispered. 'We have to be. Glidd gave us our freedom. We must use it well.'

Gently she prised his hand from her arm and placed in it Glidd's belt buckle, which had been found with the Sleeper's broken caskets.

About Moyra Caldecott

Moyra Caldecott was born in Pretoria, South Africa in 1927, and moved to London in 1951. She married Oliver Caldecott and raised three children. She has degrees in English and Philosophy and an M.A. in English Literature.

Moyra Caldecott has earned a reputation as a novelist who writes as vividly about the adventures and experiences to be encountered in the inner realms of the human consciousness as she does about those in the outer physical world. To Moyra, reality is multidimensional.

For more information about Moyra and her books, please visit www.moyracaldecott.co.uk.

www.ingramcontent.com/pod-product-compliance
Lightning Source LLC
Chambersburg PA
CBHW032118020726
47494CB00007BA/2127